Aimless Fear

Rod Griffiths

Black Pear Press

Wolf Press
A Black Pear Press imprint
www.blackpear.net

Front cover design: Lois Parker

Back cover photograph: Geoff Robinson 2020zoom

DEDICATION

**Dedicated to Lois who not only encouraged me
to write, but also put up with it.**

Other works by Rod Griffiths
Side Effect – Like a Rag Doll Falling
ISBN 978-0-9565263-0-4

ACKNOWLEDGMENTS

With acknowledgements to the fine folk who run NaNoWriMo each year. It may seem like a daft idea to write a novel in a month, but it is fun and it got the first draft of this book written.

CHAPTER 1

The Jumble Sale

'Fear is aimless,' the priest's voice echoed from the loudspeaker, 'but evil has direction, so we know which way to face when we fight it. Fear is harder to resist.' He paused, looking confused and glanced at the paper he was holding. Where did that come from? he thought. I don't remember writing that. He looked out at the assembled parishioners and grinned sheepishly.

'I seem to be speaking from the wrong notes.'

A ripple of laughter swept across the crowd.

'What I am afraid of,' he said, getting back into his stride, 'is the church roof leaking, so I ask you to support this jumble sale, to spend as much as you are able to afford and help us raise money to fix the roof.'

He paused again and smiled at the crowd.

'I declare the sale open.' He stopped, visibly relieved and stepped off the platform to a smattering of cheers and desultory applause.

'What was all that about?,' whispered his wife.

'I don't know. It just suddenly came to me out of thin air. I couldn't think what to say next.'

'You just said you had the wrong notes.'

'That was an excuse. I had the right notes, but something else came out. I don't know where it came from. It's rather a good line, I'll have to use it sometime, pity it has nothing to do with the jumble sale. Anyway, it's open, so no more speeches 'til Sunday.'

Five seconds later a small boy, aged about six, came at him, running full pelt and screaming. The vicar knelt down and caught him.

'Bogey man, there's a bogey man. Run, run away.' The boy twisted in the priest's grasp, trying to look over his shoulder and break free at the same time.

'Run.' He struggled against the black cloth, his breath coming in gasps.

'Look at me,' said Reverend Ashton, 'look at me. Do you see this white collar? That's a special collar that stops bogey men. You're safe with me.'

The boy stopped screaming and twisting for a second and reached out to feel the collar, then collapsed into great heaving sobs.

'What's your name?'

The question was answered with another sob and nothing more. The vicar looked up at his wife.

'We'd better try to find his mother.'

'You mean I'd better find his mother; you'll have to keep him safe with your magic collar. Something has obviously scared him silly. We haven't got any ghost attractions or horror museums have we?'

'No.'

The child continued to sob and gave no indication of his identity.

'I'll get them to turn the PA system back on.'

'OK. I'll take him for a drink.' Turning back to the boy he said, 'Would you like some hot chocolate? They have some in the tent over there. Shall we go and find some?'

The vicar stood up and, holding the child's hand, tried to move in the direction of the refreshment tent, but the child was having none of it. With his other arm wrapped resolutely around the vicar's leg forward motion was impossible.

'Perhaps I'd better carry you, I expect all that running has made you tired.'

He lifted him into his arms and they set off. A minute later, the child had a smear of chocolate around his mouth and the vicar's wife's voice boomed out over the fair. Once the chocolate had done its work, he volunteered his name.

'So, Dwayne, tell me about this bogey man. We'd better look out for him and make sure he doesn't scare any more children.'

'Big black shape, trying to grab me.'

'How tall was he?'

'Bigger than you.'

'What was he wearing?'

'Black, too black to see, black like inside a cupboard.' He shuddered.

'Well done. I think that will do for now. Joyce will find your mummy soon.'

The announcement boomed out again and as the sound died away, another scream rang out.

* * *

Mrs Jacobs was tending her stall next to the refreshment tent, separated by a few millimetres of canvas from Dwayne and the vicar. She heard the scream and it made her heart flutter; the last thing she needed. She'd had the angina for six months and the doctor said that there was not a lot that could be done at her age. She was not to know that she had a rather old fashioned doctor; a modern one would have had her in hospital within the week, with angiograms for starters, a stent for the main course, and Statins for the rest of her life as dessert.

Mrs Jacobs had resigned herself to the idea that her time had come. This jumble sale was her last hurrah; she was determined to sell as many of her ancient possessions as she could. The more money she made for the church, she figured, the better her chances in the afterlife.

Her stall was crammed. She'd spent three hours getting ready, with occasional breaks to suck one of those nitro-glycerine tablets that the doctor said would help. She felt the cold more these days, the doctor said it was the heart failure, so she brought a little stove to keep her warm. A camping stove really; she'd had it for years, since the children were small. It ran from a cylinder of propane connected to an ancient rubber hose. She used an old shopping trolley to move the whole thing and the rubber hose was long enough to reach to the stove on the table, high enough that she didn't have to bend with the boiling water. The tube was getting a little stiff these days but she had no idea where she could get another, John had done that sort of thing. If she handled it with care it would probably last her. She warmed her hands as the water boiled. How many more brews would she drink before her heart gave out? Silly thoughts, she said to herself, make the tea and get ready for the customers. She felt a little guilty about the stove, it probably wasn't allowed, but if it helped raise money for the church surely no one would mind. She might even be able to sell the stove.

The table in front of her was covered in small ornaments, some silver, some porcelain, all priced far too cheap for what they were. A large mirror stood at one side, surrounded by an ornamental frame. It had been in her bedroom for fifty years but it had to go. She didn't like to see herself any more. Even in the dim light of her bedroom the blue tinge to her lips was depressing. It wasn't so bad in the morning but climbing the stairs at night was such an effort. Balancing the mirror on the table today had been a struggle but luckily a young man had offered to help her. He'd said very kind things about her stall and taken her picture standing with some of her ornaments and jewellery.

She was halfway through her second cup of tea when she heard the scream. It came from a young man forty yards away. With her dimming eyesight she struggled to recognise him; was it the young man with the blue eyes who'd helped her an hour ago?

* * *

For the young man it looked like being a great day, the old girl had a mass of good stuff. OK, he might have to buy it, but this was a jumble sale and nothing was going to cost more than pennies. Selling it on was the trick and you got the best price if you could demonstrate provenance. She was on her last legs, she'd said as much, so all he had to do was pick up the best pieces and then pass her off as his granny. Getting her to pose with him for a picture was the hard part. Standing next to the jumble stall would have looked hopeless and been a dead give away to anyone in the trade. He was very proud of the trick; he'd casually propped his phone on the stall with the movie camera running and then asked her about a grave thirty yards away.

She couldn't resist talking to him about her husband who'd been buried there for ten years. It might look like a lucky guess that the name was the same, but in a small village the odds were in his favour. It had taken half an hour to find someone who knew her name and another fifteen minutes to find the grave, plus two more minutes to find something unusual about a nearby grave. Once he had that he was all set to capture a neat little movie segment of the two of them walking together across the graveyard. Perfectly innocent; it could have been taken by a relative, or a friend. Clip out a few stills and he'd have a family album which was exactly what he needed.

The best thing to do at these sorts of sales was to be early and lend a helping hand setting up. Half an hour of apparently aimless wandering and you could usually find all the items that were worth having. On this occasion, she was the only show in town. Give her a few minutes without any customers and then move in. What could be easier?

Somewhere in the back of his mind there was a tiny worry. If she turned to the right and the light caught her hair, she reminded him of his aunty; not a lot, but a hint and that disturbed him. Guilt wasn't a thing that troubled him much but occasionally it slowed him down for a moment.

He wasn't a bad person. Conning people to part with their antiques for a fraction of what they were worth wasn't actually a crime. They didn't have to sell them, they could get a valuation of their own, so stop worrying about it, he said to himself. Think positive. Better to be conned by me than by someone else. After all, I do go to some trouble to figure out a tempting offer. My profit is simply a fee to cover the cost of acquiring my superior knowledge.

He still dithered and hesitated, trying to find his focus. Maybe that hesitation caused the problem, maybe it was something else. If anyone had been watching they would have seen his expression change, his brows furrowed as he became confused and then agitated and rapidly descended into some inner turmoil.

The anxiety turned into panic. He somehow became shorter, shrinking into his shell. His hands tensed for a fight, his head turning rapidly, randomly, looking for some threat. If anyone had happened to glance in his direction they would probably have been frightened themselves. They'd see a man cowering in the middle of the space between the stalls and tables of the jumble sale, apparently desperate to avoid some terror. They would probably be convinced that a tree was about to fall on their head or a runaway truck about to carve through the assembled parishioners.

Then he ran and screamed, or did he scream and then run? By the time everyone turned to look it made little difference; head down, in short stuttering strides he was picking up speed, weaving and dodging as if going for a touchdown and yelling incoherently. In another twenty yards and going flat out, his eyes fixated on the big ornate mirror that only half an hour ago he'd helped set up.

Now he was shouting something, hurling abuse at the mirror. None of the witnesses could say what it was. It may have been, 'Get away from me,' but his voice had become so guttural and staccato that no one could make any sense of the words.

There was no time to think about it, stop him, or do anything before he leapt at the mirror. He must have been three feet off the ground when he hit it, full on, head down, with one fist extended. On any other day the leap might have been admired, maximum points for style and speed, but this wasn't the village sports day.

She saw him coming, though at that distance he was a blur until he got closer. When he was close enough to recognise, all she could see was the terror and fear in his eyes. The onlookers saw her step backwards and clutch at her throat, fighting for breath and then begin to pitch forwards as the mirror shattered and the two of them were enveloped in a mass of flying glass.

If there had been a slow motion video it might have looked even worse. His fist smashed into the mirror, breaking a foot of glass at the top into three pieces and slowing him down. One of the shards chopped into his left wrist, severing the radial artery, not a fatal injury, but more was to come.

His blood spurted, spraying into her face and eyes. Maybe that was the deathblow, the shock and the temporary blindness being too much to cope with? Or perhaps her heart had stopped before he even struck the mirror? Blood freewheels around the circulation for no more than a few seconds after the last heartbeat and the brain runs out of oxygen a few seconds after that. To say in which split second she lost consciousness would be beyond medical science, but she crumpled forwards, her torso collapsing on to the table before her legs gave way and the whole structure started to topple backwards.

The initial impact slowed the young man's momentum so that he began to fall more vertically, but he was well into the mirror now. The large remaining piece of the glass sliced into his neck. Gory movies talk about going for the jugular but that's not the real killer. Right next to the vein is the carotid artery, almost as big as your little finger and full of blood pumping hard enough to shoot clean over your head. A frightened man, running full tilt, has an even higher pressure and his heart is beating twice as fast. Every heart beat pushes out enough blood to fill a couple of espresso cups, not a massive amount, but a hundred heartbeats a minute is a lot of espressos and your whole blood volume could be gone in a minute. He was beyond saving by the time he had crashed on to the remains of the table, but it didn't end there.

The elderly woman had knocked her little stove forwards off the table and one of the remaining chunks of the mirror sliced into the old and brittle gas pipe as it fell. The pipe was severed completely and sprang away from the table, thrashing around with what remained of its elasticity for a second before coming to rest on the floor, right alongside the fabric of the refreshment tent, gushing gas as the cylinder emptied. Two dead bodies and a pile of glass and smashed ornaments were plenty enough to make sure that no one saw the pipe and anyway, how were they to know that the cloud of propane was expanding into the refreshment tent just behind the burners that were heating lunch?

The sheet of fire enveloped the vicar and Dwayne as his mother got to the tent with the vicar's wife. All she saw was her boy sitting on the preacher's knee as the flames expanded around them.

Dwayne's mother froze for a second and then started to rush towards her son. She was swept aside as everyone in the tent ran for the door. The stampede almost crushed several people but those who fell were lucky in a way. As they lay on the ground the explosion from the second gas bottle heating lunch went over their head, along with the chicken curry.

Everyone ran—a stampede flattening stalls, trampling everything in its path until they reached open ground and lost momentum. When they talked afterwards in quiet huddles, or later still in police statements, they spoke of terror, of some nameless fear that enveloped them, quite out of proportion to the size of the explosion. Some simply went home, some sat in the safety of their cars taking relief in a metal box to keep out the waves of panic that had swept through the whole crowd. Some, to their credit, turned and went back to see what help they could give.

The lone man from St John Ambulance stayed at his post but the crowd had run the other way. There were some who had stopped in their tracks, interrupted in their flight by injuries, twisted ankles, grazed knees and small burns; nothing serious, but enough to take their minds off running. Over the next half an hour the lone paramedic patched them up.

The village bobby had arrived on the scene a few minutes before the explosion. He had a reputation for lurking, for somehow being invisible until he appeared where least expected. In a quiet way he had been congratulating himself on spotting a well-known con man; a smart young man with blue eyes and a charming manner. He was keeping his distance, watching to see who was the likely victim and then all hell broke loose and now the conman was lying under a sheet of canvas with three other bodies. In the movies the police are always equipped with flashing lights and special police tape. They seal off the scene and put a tent around the bodies, but it's hard to get all that stuff on a bicycle.

'That'll have to do,' said Sam Diglis to no one in

particular. 'I'll have to organise forensics and the squad from division, as well as coroners and inquests and all that. What was that kid running from?' He stopped himself mumbling, straightened his shoulders and took out his notebook.

CHAPTER 2

Sam Diglis

There was no video of the carnage at the jumble sale, no pictures, just a smoking mess and four bodies. A public appeal to try to find any snaps that might have been taken was issued but none came forward and Sam Diglis had no regrets about that. Ten years ago, a videotape had marked his life forever and he didn't need another. Video doesn't lie but it doesn't tell the whole story. The camera catches the scene but it never picks up the smell of it, or what happened before. You can't see behind the picture or off the sides. You can't see the faces of the people with their backs to you and, unless it has a microphone, you don't hear a thing.

Sam never could square that videotape with what went on in his head. The images came from a camera situated on the side of the building; not the clearest film, not like your modern stuff, but it had been clear enough to get him a medal. All you saw initially was the street and if you looked very carefully, comparing the still images, it was just possible to tell that the light varied. The clever lads back at the lab worked out the frequency and figured out that it was the flashing light from the burglar alarm but that was off camera. The deafening noise was not on the tape, but you could hear it on the recording as Colin radioed back to HQ; hard to hear anything else. Maybe it was because of the noise that he forgot to turn the microphone off, so the deafening wailing was recorded for the next five minutes.

They'd only been a street away when they got the

call and they were travelling in the right direction, so Colin put his foot down, took the corner in a four-wheel slide, clipped a dustbin with the back wing and screamed down the middle of the street to come to a rubber-burning stop, right in front of the building. That wasn't on the camera footage, not until the front of the car appeared, but it did pick up the crooks running out.

People say things like "time stood still" but it's a trick of the mind. Research has shown that the brain can shift all its processing power to one activity. More attention on one thing makes it feel as though there is more time to get it done, whatever it is. Even if all you are doing is watching something terrible happen in front of you, it still feels as though time has slowed down. Athletes train themselves so that they can shut out extraneous detail, concentrate totally on one crucial task, one poetic movement; they call it focus.

Anyone can do it, but athletes do it deliberately. For ordinary mortals time only slows down when something makes it happen, like some extraordinary event such as the girl next door kissing you for the first time or the bloke across the street shooting at you.

Two men ran out, both medium build, a big, black, loose leather coat on one of them, like in that movie; the other in jeans and a sweater. Both of them were wearing balaclavas so you could only see their eyes and noses, enough to tell they were white. Both were wearing gloves and the sweater guy was carrying a bag.

Colin climbed out of the driver's door and shouted, 'Police!', which was bloody obvious because both Colin and Sam were in uniform. 'Stop right there,' he yelled. You could just about make that out on the voice tape, over the noise of the alarm. The door shuts with a clunk and Sam's door slams straight after, so the rest of the recording from inside the car has only the muffled sound of the alarm, right up until the gunshots.

The one with the coat pulled the piece and fired at

Colin as Sam was coming around the front of the car. On the video, you can catch a glimpse of Colin's shoulder as he falls. The crook wasn't much of a shot; the bullet caught Colin in the right knee and he fell. The next shot was aimed higher but Colin was already on the way down, so the second one went over his shoulder and took out the window in the back door and ended up in the car's upholstery.

Three frames further on and Sam was past the front of the car and visible on the camera. He stepped forward and held up his hand, as if he were stopping traffic. You could only see his back. He took two more steps forward and stopped. Four frames later the voice recorder picks up something, but it's muffled. With the car doors closed and the alarm going off, not even the boffins could make it out and they tried; tried for a week.

Sam's never said—claims he can't remember—something about more police coming and not being able to get away. He stood like a statue with his arm up. All you can see on the video is his back, but he must have looked quite a figure—six foot two, dark uniform and shiny buttons, facing the man with the gun. The stand off lasted a couple of seconds and whatever he said, it had the right effect on the guy in the sweater because he grabbed his mate's hand, laid the gun on the ground and it was all over. It happened very fast. The man in the coat looked like he was going to shoot; his eyes were focussed on Sam. The sweater guy is hard to read, his lips were moving, shouting something, but that's just another muffled blur on the tape. He was moving fast and the balaclava covered enough of his face that the lip readers couldn't make it out.

Sam got a medal. "With no regard to his own safety he stood up to an armed assailant who had already shot one officer," the citation said.

At the trial it came out that sweater guy didn't know

that the thug in the leather coat was a fantasist whose flat was full of violent video games and guns, mostly replicas if the truth were known, but the pictures shown at the trial had the right effect on the judge and jury. Sweater guy must have sized up the situation very fast, realised that they wouldn't get away with it and grabbed the gun. It paid off at the trial and he got out years before his accomplice.

Colin had a permanent limp, which was worse when the weather was cold and enough to get him off driving. It was enough to get him off lots of things over the years, but he always looked a fine figure of a man behind his desk and he was never short of a drink or two from new recruits.

The video in Sam's head looked quite different, a lot longer for a start and one way or another, it played for the next ten years. It begins the same, the radio call, putting on the lights and siren, fifty miles an hour around the block, wondering if Colin's driving was up to it and sliding to a halt in front of the flashing light.

He heard Colin report in as he opened the car door and the air was filled with the wail of the alarm. At first glance, it wasn't obvious what the premises were. An anonymous building that could afford a bloody loud alarm. Could be a wages snatch from an office, or one of those exclusive jewellers shops where they only let you in by appointment, or could it be a false alarm? As the car stopped, his favourite theory was a false alarm and he almost said as much to Colin.

Then the men ran out and the balaclavas were a dead give away. Sam heard Colin shout and then the idiot in the big coat pulled a gun. He only caught sight of it in his peripheral vision as he was looking down at the pavement, mentally cursing Colin for parking badly.

'I could have snapped my Achilles tendon,' Sam thought as he half stepped on the kerbstone.

Sam had just got his balance and stepped forward in

front of the car as he heard the first shot. Still moving forward, he saw Colin stagger sideways and fall as his knee gave way and then the second shot smashed into the car window.

When you get a burst of adrenaline your heart speeds up, but the adrenalin comes out of a gland somewhere down in your abdomen and it only shoves the stuff into your bloodstream when it gets a signal from your brain. After that, the hormone has to go all the way around your body and be taken up by the muscles before anything happens. That sequence takes about half a minute on a good day. When you are scared out of your mind the brain does its thing immediately. It tells the heart to beat faster, which winds up the reflexes to top speed and it tells the adrenal gland to pull its finger out so the whole thing can keep going. The brain does the clever stuff about ignoring everything except the task in hand, so you don't waste time and energy thinking about the weather when you need to dodge a bullet.

Sam's brain had got through all the preliminary work as they rounded the corner and the crash of the bin hitting the rear wing spooked him. Sam was looking forwards, the flashing alarm had just entered his vision, so the last thing he was expecting was a bang behind him, followed by a rattling cacophony as the rubbish scattered down the road.

By the time he took those two steps around the car he was already flooded with adrenaline, so the sound of the shot put him into the next gear after overdrive. The one clever thing his brain did manage was to tell his voice to say, 'Armed police are on their way.'

He never owned up to saying that. In the cold light of day it sounded like a bluff but it was true, in a sense. Once the shots had been heard at HQ and maybe when they heard Colin yell, 'I'm shot,' then they would be bound to send an armed response car. Bound to. So it was true, they were on their way—sort of.

Maybe it was a good idea that his brain raised his arm as though he were directing traffic. Not exactly likely to catch a bullet but it at least put a new picture in the gunman's face, maybe made him think for a second. Who knows?

The main thing Sam's brain did was to make his body freeze. The robbers may have thought he was going to do something, charge at them perhaps, but in reality, all Sam could do was stand there with his hand up. Some animals freeze when they are full of adrenalin. Keeping dead still if you're a rabbit caught in headlights is suicide, but it makes sense if you're a mouse in a field trying to stop a buzzard seeing you.

Sam froze like a mouse, but he was in the middle of the road like a rabbit and time stood still. His brain did a good job at keeping out all the distractions but his inner clock went faster, which made the whole thing last longer.

On the video it's all over in a few seconds, but in Sam's mind, it lasted an age. It got him a medal and that made it worse, much worse. It produced countless opportunities for people to remind him about that day and any mention of it made Sam feel as if he'd been frozen in panic ever since.

He had a medal for bravery but being frozen to the spot isn't brave, it's bloody stupid. It could put your colleagues in danger, put you in danger for sure and make you a sitting duck for a bloke in a big black coat with a gun.

Sam got the medal because all his bosses saw was the video, but that long drawn out second changed his life forever. Before that second he was a keen young cop; bright, on the ball and expected to go far. After that second he was a loner; a loner with a medal, but a loner.

Deep in his heart he didn't trust himself to work

with other people. He volunteered for jobs that he could do on his own. People put it down to his legendary bravery. He wasn't unapproachable. He'd be happy to drink a beer with the rest any day but it was Colin that they bought drinks for. Sam saved a life and somehow that set him apart. There was something in him that no one could get through to. Everyone put it down to his steely resolve.

They had psychologists of course. Being shot at got you a free pass to that sort of thing but it did no good. They tried, oh yes they tried, and maybe they helped him decide what to do because they made him think. Think and think and think, but always when he said he had frozen, that he couldn't have moved a muscle if he tried, he knew they didn't really believe him. They put it down to modesty; he could see it in their eyes.

Sam had standards. He'd always wanted to be a good cop, wanted to be the best, was bright enough to be on top of all the modern science but where did it get you if you didn't trust yourself?

Eventually he found a village that needed a policeman, a visible bobby on the beat; it came with it's own house and a regulation bicycle. There was a motorbike too. He was rather proud of the way that he had persuaded the higher ups that he needed an off-road bike.

'You can't catch poachers on the roads.'

Over the ten years after the shooting Sam gradually transformed himself into the local village bobby, looking after a patch that only warranted one police officer and where there was virtually no crime at all.

It was barely a full-time job but the medal gave him some leverage, so he arranged a day each week to help the clever boys in the labs. They were happy to have him, to take a small gleam of reflected glory. It kept him up-to-date and satisfied some of his need to contribute and do well. One way or another it should have been a happy life; apart from the nightmares.

Sam did good work after the jumble sale exploded. He calmed everyone down, took statements, got the forensic people working, alerted the coroner and, while looking disappointed about it, confirmed that there were no useful videos or pictures. He'd already recognised the blue-eyed young man, so he briefed the detectives and set them trying to make sense of that last desperate run. Sam concentrated on picking up the pieces in the village, keeping up the act as good old Sam Diglis—brave and dependable—just what the village needed.

CHAPTER 3

Stampede

Cows weigh about a thousand pounds, about half as much as a car. Cows eat grass and precious little else and to digest the stuff, they have to sit around and let all sorts of chemistry go on in their stomachs, breaking down cellulose and turning it into sugar. Most people don't know that cellulose and starch are almost the same chemical. They are sugar molecules bonded together in long chains and the difference is the bonds that hold them. Whether you can digest them depends on having the right enzyme to break those bonds and release the sugar. Cellulose holds plants together, whereas starch stores energy. Unlike humans, animals like rabbits and cows can digest cellulose because they have some enzymes that can break down the cellulose into sugar. Strictly speaking, they borrow those enzymes from microbes living in their intestine, so the process takes a while. Hardly surprising then that cows spend a lot of time sitting around waiting for all that chemistry to happen.

Despite weighing half a ton and in many cases having horns sticking out of their heads, the main images of cows are peaceful. There are poems, paintings and no end of romantic stuff about peaceful cows in peaceful meadows, England's green and pleasant land, and similar. The last thing you ever expect in the English countryside is a cattle stampede like those lethal affairs that only happen in old-fashioned Westerns.

In the movies, the cattle are Texas Longhorns,

particularly fearsome looking beasts with horns a few feet across. Movie producers focus on the horns but spare a thought for the hooves; there are four of them per cow and if one lands on you there's half a ton behind it.

Cows must like each other because they always seem happy moving in a herd, cuddled up close together. Stand at a farm gate and look at cows and there's a good chance that they'll be overcome with curiosity and come trundling over to see what you are about. In some ways it's endearing, all that curiosity. Fortunately, it is usually tinged with shyness, so when they get about six feet away, they are overcome with embarrassment and stop in their tracks, staring at you while being shoved forward by their sisters who were a bit slow trundling across the field and haven't yet got close enough to be shy.

Newcomers to cows can get worried by the initial enthusiastic charge and may be tempted to run for it. This would be a mistake because if you run, they stay curious and keep following you. If all they can see is your fleeing back, then the shyness moment never sets in and the herd keeps trundling forwards.

None of those fears bothered Farmer Alsop's mind as he watched the herd pound across the field. In many ways it was a magnificent sight. If it had been Texas, like in the movies, there would have been a cloud of dust and bright sunshine to add to the drama but this was England, green and damp. Anxiety only began to cross his mind in the last few yards.

Most estimates put cows' top speed at a little under 20 miles per hour. If a car hits you at that speed you stand a good chance of survival, hence why we have 20 mph speed limits around schools. A cow travelling at that speed is more dangerous than a car because of its horns and hooves. Cows don't have a safety rating and no one has ever stood a crash test dummy in front of fifty stampeding cows. The first few crashed into the gate. A five bar gate is a solid structure but if it is hit hard by several half ton animals it won't last long. Those sorts of gates have mortise joints but the wood weathers and the glue cracks; bend the bars enough and the joints will spring apart. The top bar came off, one end swinging in a wide arc that caught Ralph Alsop on the back of his head. He had already turned to run, when he realised that some of the cows were going to come straight on and the gate might not hold. He set off for the safety of the stone walls of the farmyard. He never made it. The blow on his head didn't knock him out but he did lose his footing and slid down on to one knee.

Cows don't usually trample on people, they dodge around them, but when there are a dozen of them in a line and others alongside and behind them, there is no escape. Ralph was flattened in a second. A leg hit his right shoulder and knocked him sideways and then there were hooves all over his back. There were fifty cows in the herd but probably no more than half a dozen actually trampled on him. His arms and legs were torn and bruised but those injuries were survivable. The real damage was the left side of his chest. A cow's hoof is only a few inches across, about the size of a fist, but with half a ton attached can cause serious damage. Hooves caught the back of his chest twice and smashed his ribs in several places. Another one got him further down and broke the lower ribs, sending splinters of bone into his spleen and left kidney.

When you breathe, your diaphragm moves down and your ribs swing outwards. The two things together increase the volume in your chest so the air pressure falls and air is sucked in. Ralph's diaphragm moved, and if he'd been conscious it would have hurt, but the suction didn't happen because as the undamaged ribs swung outwards the smashed bits sucked in. The result was that hardly any air went in or out. The only way to survive an injury like that is for air to be blown into your lungs by a ventilator or by a person doing mouth-to-mouth first aid. Neither a machine nor a person was available as Ralph lay in the mud after the cows had gone by.

Luckily, his right lung was still OK, so a little air going into that one did some good, but the left one, under the smashed section of ribs, was battered and bleeding inside and wasn't helping Ralph's body get in air. Ralph was in a bad way. He was almost unconscious, every breath causing severe pain and barely getting enough oxygen to survive.

Below his diaphragm his ruptured spleen was quietly bleeding into his abdomen. If a hoof had caught his head and knocked him cold, it might have been better. Where he was, he had no chance of survival and not enough breath to shout for help.

In the farmyard the stampeding herd was tearing the place apart. Solid walls surrounded Ralph's yard. Those that came behind trapped the leading cows and all were driven by some nameless urge to charge onwards as if the devil himself were at their heels. They smashed into equipment, wrecking everything in their path and bellowing frantically. Ellen, Ralph's wife, came running out of the house. Fortunately, she was the other side of the wall. Initially astonished at the chaos, she sensed something of the fear driving the animals and became even more anxious when she could see no sign of Ralph. She shouted and screamed but knew she had no chance of making herself heard over the din. Hoping that Ralph was not in the yard, she back tracked towards the fields and followed the trail of trampled mud, so that five minutes later she found him.

She tried to move him, tried to help him breath but got nowhere. He still had a thin pulse. Her tears fell on his face as she blew some air into his lungs, desperately trying to remember her first aid lessons. His colour improved slightly but how long could she keep this up? Then she remembered that she'd come out without her phone. She raced back to the house. The cows were still crashing around in the yard and showed no sign of calming down from whatever had sent them crazy. She found the phone and, as she rushed back across the mud to the field, she dialled 999 for an ambulance. Ellen sat cradling Ralph in her arms, trying to help him breath, trying to comfort him and praying for the ambulance to hurry.

He died in her arms a few minutes before the two paramedics struggled through the mud to find them.

They worked on him for a few minutes, put a tube down his throat and pumped him with oxygen, shocked his heart, and tried to get it going again, but it was too late and they had no way of knowing that half his blood volume had leaked out of his ruptured spleen and was sloshing around his abdomen. That was a exciting discovery awaiting the pathologist, who could at least tell the coroner that there was no way that Ralph could have survived. He in turn reassured the paramedics that they had done all they could.

Out of respect, they put him on a stretcher and took him back to the farmhouse. They laid him on a sheet on the front room floor. Out of the mud and lying there, he looked at peace.

'We can't take him to the hospital, it needs the doctor to certify him as dead and then the coroner will decide what to do. Sorry love, it's procedure. We'll call the doctor for you.'

When they had left she ventured back to the farmyard. The cattle had stopped charging but the noise and confusion was still considerable. Every door was broken, the milking shed was a wreck and the metal gate that led to the road was buckled, but thankfully it had held. A quick glance showed that at least a dozen cows were dead or dying. Lying where they had fallen, some were moaning and bellowing, which did nothing to keep the others quiet. A few had turned and made their way back out to the field behind the house but most were clustered in shocked huddles making similar noises to their fallen sisters, almost as though they were crying for help.

Ellen stared at the scene for five minutes, tears pouring down her face, and then turned back to the house. It took several minutes to get the vet to understand what had happened and another twenty before he arrived, bringing his colleague, Joe, with him. Working cautiously, walking along the top of the walls, not daring to venture into the yard itself, they gradually persuaded the uninjured cows out into the field before closing the metal gate and parking a tractor in front of it to make sure that the herd stayed out of the yard. It didn't take long to decide that the cows on the floor had no chance. Killing them where they lay was the only choice and then the bodies were scooped up with the digger and placed on to a trailer where a tarpaulin was dragged over them.

'I'll arrange to have them collected and disposed of. I'm sorry there's nothing else I can do.'

The vet stood looking at Ellen for a minute.

'Is there someone who can come over? You look like you could do with company, or shall I call the doctor?'

'The paramedics called him already, but what can he do? Better if you could send someone who wants to buy a farm.' She wiped away a tear.

'What happened?' she said, 'why would they do that?'

He shook his head.

'I've no idea. I've never seen anything like it. Something must have set them off. I wondered if it was rustlers or something like that but there's no sign that anyone's been in the field. I've looked at the other beasts and they all look normal. I'll let Sam Diglis know, in case he's heard something or there's been other incidents.'

'What can Sam do?'

'I'm not sure,' said the vet, backing away slightly. 'He sees people in sad and difficult times and he has experience. He might be able to help.'

Ellen shrugged, holding her hands up in a helpless gesture that said, I've lost control of everything, send the doctor, send Sam, do what you like, I don't care.

As the vet got to the door, she called him back.

'Are the cows healthy, can I sell them? Is it safe to sell them?'

The vet turned back towards her, started to say something and then stopped, thinking, caught out by the question. Eventually he said, 'I didn't see anything but who knows? Maybe the best thing is to wait a day or two, see if anything develops. I'll come over tomorrow and check them all over.'

'Would anyone buy a herd that killed a farmer?' she said. 'Would you?'

The question hung in the air as the vet hesitated.

'I'll have to sell,' she said. 'I can't milk them, the yard's a wreck, the milking shed is a wreck. I can't milk them in the field, I'd be too scared. It'll take a week to clear up this mess and they'll all be dry by then.' She sank into the chair, holding her head in her hands.

'I'll see what I can do,' he said. 'Give me an hour. I'll call the doc as well. Will you be alright? Joe can stay if you like.'

'Go,' she said. 'Just go, do what you think is best.'

He closed the door gently behind him and turned to Joe.

'Come on, let's get out of here.'

'She does need the doctor whatever she says, she'll

have to have a death certificate.'

'Sure, but it'll have to go to the coroner, there'll be an inquest, but the doc can set it going and maybe get her a social worker or something.'

CHAPTER 4

The Crash

Paperwork from the two disasters on his patch still covered Sam's desk. It was already five thirty and the thought of what to cook for supper was beginning to intrude on his concentration. The phone rang.

'Sam, there's been a crash on The Avenue, don't know the details, they've hit a tree, ambulance has been called. Don't know any more than that.'

'Hit a tree? It's a straight road, did they fall asleep?'

'No idea, Sam, the call came from the switchboard via a triple-nine call. Someone made the call so you may have a witness, haven't heard anything from the ambulance yet, they're still on their way I think.'

'OK, I'll get down there.'

Sam put the phone down and grabbed what he called his emergency food, a chocolate bar and an apple, and headed for the car.

Two minutes later he swung round the roundabout and on to The Avenue. Two hundred yards ahead on the other side of the road he could see the flashing lights of an ambulance eerily illuminating the shape of a car, sideways, half on the pavement. Mentally noting, dark blue or black, some sort of sports coupe, he swung across the road, parking at an angle to cover two of the four lanes and left his blue light flashing. As he opened the boot to take out his RTA kit, he saw more blue lights coming down the road in the opposite direction. Good, the traffic boys are here, he thought, as he walked down the road towards the wrecked car. As his eyes accommodated to the light, he could see two figures sitting in the back of the ambulance. One of the paramedics was doing his stuff, shining lights in the patients' eyes and taking their blood pressure. He looked up as Sam came into view.

'Those two from the car?'

The driver nodded.

'They look OK.'

'Yeah, we only just got here, but they both walked to our vehicle.'

'Any witnesses? Someone called 999.'

'Another car. I told him to park around the corner, he'll be waiting for you.'

'Right you are, hang on to these two unless you need to rush them to hospital, I won't be long.'

Sam walked along the road. About thirty yards from the ambulance he found a massive skid mark across the road and on to the pavement. Following the line of it led him to a tree in the hedge with a huge chunk torn out of it.

'Bloody hell,' he said under his breath, 'they hit that at a bit of a whack, must have bounced off and landed up where they are now.' He took a tape measure from his bag and ran it over the skid mark. He drew a quick sketch and noted the number, put the book and measuring tape back in his bag and walked round the corner to find a white car parked neatly; as he arrived the driver got out. Middle-aged white male, glasses, suit, tie, hopefully a reliable witness, thought Sam. At least he'd look the part in court if it comes to that.

'I'm Sam Diglis, police. Are you happy talking here or do you want to sit in the car?'

'This'll do fine.'

'OK, I know it's never easy, everything happens so fast, but try to tell me in your own words what happened. Do you mind if I tape it? Saves me having to stop you all the time because I can't write fast enough.'

The man nodded as Sam turned on the machine.

Sam listened for five minutes.

'So to summarise, this blue car overtook you and immediately after he'd got past, he swerved back into your lane, came right across the road, hit the curb, flew up in the air, hit the tree in the hedge, spun around completely in mid air and came to rest further down the road, half facing back the way he'd come. You slammed on your brakes and managed to avoid hitting him. From what I've gathered he must have been going quite a bit faster than you because he'd gone far enough down the road that it gave you room to stop. After that, you called 999 on your mobile and parked back here when the ambulance came. Did you talk to the people in the blue car?'

'Yes, well, sort of. I rushed up expecting to find them half dead or at least knocked out, but they weren't. They were both conscious, looked a bit shaken; well, very shaken, pale and looking shocked. I told them I'd call an ambulance and that was it really.'

'Did they say anything?'

'I think I said, are you OK, does it hurt anywhere, any bones broken? They both said they were OK and the driver said, did you see that car?, or something like that. I thought it best not to get into any of that, so I let them be and dialled 999. After that I called my wife. I felt a bit shaken up myself, so I stayed on the phone to her. She was worried, obviously, and I think I kept talking so I didn't have to talk to them. I was a bit annoyed, probably adrenaline and nerves I guess, but I didn't want to say anything I might regret.'

'What sort of thing might that be?'

'Well you've seen the car. I don't know what it is exactly, but it's some sort of souped-up sports job isn't it? These people tearing about the place in cars like that. I didn't want to get into an argument. No point in saying what the hell do you think you were doing? It would only get me into trouble, so I kept talking to my wife until the ambulance came. They asked me to park here, so I was out of the way I think; let them get on with their work.'

'Did you see any other cars or people? I need to find out if there any other witnesses.'

'I didn't see anyone else, or any other cars. There was a dog, but you can't get a statement from a dog, I guess.'

'Tell me about the dog.'

'When I stopped it was rushing around barking. Odd really, I thought it was trailing a lead, as though it had pulled away from its owner. I didn't take much notice; I was more worried about the people in the blue car. When I got out of the car it ran off through the hedge, I guess it must have come from one of the houses.'

'Mr. Wilson, you've been very helpful, thanks. Can I ask you to hang on a few minutes while I talk briefly to the other people?' Sam smiled. 'You'll probably want to phone your wife again.'

Sam watched him get back in his car and pick up his mobile. Around the corner the ambulance lights were still flashing as Sam walked back along the road. He looked again at the tree, took a picture of the damage with his phone and another picture of the skid marks and the damage to the kerbstone. He took out his tape measure, attached one end to the tree and started to measure along the pavement towards the wrecked car. As he unwound the tape, he heard a panting noise. Must be that dog, he thought, and looked into the hedge. Seeing nothing, he unwound another yard of tape and then another and as he did he saw a gap in the hedge, a few broken branches. The sound was louder, not panting, almost whining, but definitely a dog. He tried to see through the hedge in what was left of the evening light. He thought he could make out the shape of the dog, so he pushed his way through the twigs and undergrowth into the hedge. He was looking at the ground, uncertain what he might be treading on, when he saw a shoe. Taking out his torch, it was immediately obvious that the shoe was attached to a leg. Once he'd got through the hedge there was a body of a man lying on his back, with a dog licking his face and whimpering quietly.

Sam knelt by the body feeling for a pulse and found nothing. He held his ear by the man's mouth listening for breath and, again, heard nothing. He tore the man's shirt open and pressed his ear to his chest, listening for a heartbeat. As he pressed his ear downwards, he was shocked to feel the chest give under the pressure. He sat back on his heels, put his hand on the chest and felt the ribs buckle. It didn't take long then to notice that the man's right leg was clearly broken; the thigh simply can't bend that way. It didn't matter how hard he listened or where he put his fingers, there was no breath, no sound of a heartbeat and no pulse. He pushed the dog out of the way and tried blowing some air into the man's mouth. He saw the chest rise. He stopped blowing and the chest wall slowly fell. He tried two more times and then attempted to pump the chest. He felt more ribs crackle under his hand and there was no resistance from the chest wall. This is not what they said in class, he thought, as he tried to compress the chest to pump the heart. There was no sign of life and the chest stayed compressed.

Sam sighed, stood up, took three pictures and then picked up the dog's lead and pushed his way back through the hedge. He took pictures of the damage to the hedge and then carried on measuring the distance to the wrecked blue car. He made some notes, walking around the car, looking for dents and marks and tried to collect his thoughts.

He walked back to the ambulance and beckoned to one of the crew. Once the man was clear of the truck, he took his elbow and led him down the road until he was sure he was out of possible earshot of the ambulance.

'You'd better come and look at this.' He almost shoved the paramedic through the hedge.

As soon as he saw the body the man leapt into action but it took him only a few seconds to realise that it was hopeless.

'His chest is smashed to bits. He must have been hit by the car.' He thought about it for a second. 'We can just about get a stretcher in here. We'll take him down to the morgue and let the coroner deal with him. Do you need any more evidence from the scene?'

'I've taken some pictures; I'll take some more when you've moved him. Looks clear to me that the car impact killed him, he hasn't hit anything solid going through the hedge. We'll impound the car, there's a likely looking bump and forensics are bound to find clothes residues on it somewhere.'

'What'll you do about the two in the ambulance?'

'Are you taking them to hospital?'

'There's nothing urgent.'

'The traffic boys should be here by now, they'll probably want to arrest the driver, if we know which one was driving, and get a doctor to look at them at the station.'

They walked back to the ambulance.

'Any idea who it is?'

'There's no ID on him but there's a tag on the dog's collar, lives around the corner. I'll go and see what I can find out once we're clear here.'

'I don't envy you.'

Sam shrugged; it went with the territory.

He called Police HQ and explained the situation and made his way to the squad car that had arrived while he was in the hedge. The driver was on the radio, so Sam waited until he was clear before tapping on the window.

'Yeah?'

'Is your mate interviewing the driver?'

'They're over in the ambulance, why?'

'It's worse than it looks, there's a dead body back in the hedge, looks like the car hit him.'

'You'd better go and tell Neil. I'm waiting for a call back from a recovery truck. Shit, now we'll have to have get all the business down here.'

Sam walked over to the ambulance; the door was ajar and Neil was deep in conversation with the car driver.

The middle-aged couple sitting in the ambulance looked shaken and anxious. Sam was about to speak but Neil glanced at him and held his hand up.

Sam listened. Apparently the driver's name was Sanders and he was telling almost the same story Sam had heard from the other witness. The one different detail was his description of a black vehicle that seemed to appear from nowhere almost on their side of the road. It had no lights, seemed to be moving very fast. Sanders swerved to miss it and somehow lost control as he turned in and the next thing he knew they had hit the curb, bounced up in the air and hit the tree. The car spun around so fast that it was hard to know what was happening before they crashed back on to the road facing the wrong way.

Neil cut in.

'About this black vehicle. Could you describe it more clearly? We'll have to try to identify it, so if you can give us anything else to go on it might help.'

'It was definitely black and big, took up masses of road.'

'Big like a BMW or a Volvo, or bigger than that, like a Rolls or a Bentley, or was it a van or a truck?'

'Like those things they call Chelsea tractors,' said Mrs. Sanders, 'something like that. It was hard to make out, there was something very scary about it.' She paused for a second and shuddered. 'It sounds silly now but it was like seeing a ghost. I suppose it was because it was going so fast.'

'Did you think it was going to hit you? Is that why you swerved? It should have been on the other side of the road.'

'That's what it felt like,' said Mr. Sanders. 'After that I think we must have skidded on something. It all happened so quickly.'

I'm going to have to stop this, thought Sam.

He tapped Neil on the should.

'A word if you can, Sergeant, something you need to know.

'Not now.'

'It is important and pertinent.'

Looking irritated, Neil pushed the door further open and stepped out.

'Please wait here,' he said to the Sanders couple.

'What?'

'There's a dead body back in the hedge, smashed up badly, must have been hit by the car, my guess is you'll have to caution them.'

"What?'

'Looks like it was someone local walking his dog.' Sam turned and pointed to the dog tethered to a tree in the hedge.

'The dog's got an address tag, so I'll go and investigate, but it looks like this guy's up for Death by Dangerous Driving.'

There was a long pause. Sam watched as Neil's expression went from annoyance to relief and then to anxious concentration. Eventually he said, 'Sam isn't it? Sam Diglis?'

Sam nodded.

'Thanks, Sam, quite right. Have to do it by the book, don't want him getting off on a technicality. How did you spot the casualty.'

'Saw the dog in the hedge standing over him, the impact had knocked him clean through into the garden the other side of the hedge.'

'And he's definitely dead.'

'No doubt about it, the ambulance bloke is organising to get him to the morgue.'

'OK, I'll go and sort these two out.'

Sam listened as Neil went through the routine of cautioning Mr Sanders and arresting him on suspicion of causing death by dangerous driving.

The couple looked shocked.

Mrs sanders was the first to recover.

'I didn't see anyone. Where was this man?

'He was walking his dog on the pavement.'

'Where?'

'As far as I can tell, about ten or twenty yards up the road from where you hit the tree. When you hit the tree, he would have been on the pavement on your right hand side. It was only twilight so you should have been able to see him.'

'There was no one there when we stopped.'

'The other driver said he saw the dog running around after the crash. Did you see the dog?'

'No.'

Neil looked directly at Mrs Sanders.

'Did you see a dog? It would have been on your side of the car after you stopped.'

'I don't think I saw anything.' She stopped for a second. 'I was glad to be alive. I was looking at Tim to see if he was hurt, we were still in the car when that other driver came to see if we were alright. There wasn't a dog anywhere when we got out of the car.'

Mr Sanders, still looking very pale, said, 'We'd both just been scared out of our minds, we sat there shaking; I don't think we'd have seen Santa Claus if he'd walked by.'

Neil nodded and made a note in his book, deliberately letting the silence build some tension.

He looked up again.

'So, to summarise, you thought you saw a car, or some sort of vehicle on the other side of the road, going fast, possibly intruding into the lane in front of you, but you can't really describe it. You swerved to avoid it, even though it is a four-lane road; you may have skidded on something, but you didn't see what, then you hit a tree and didn't see anything else. How is your vision, Mr. Sanders? When did you last have an eye test?'

'My vision is fine.'

Neil nodded.

'We can't say exactly what happened until the forensic people have examined the scene and your car, which will be impounded. What we do know is that at some point after you hit the tree some part of your car struck a pedestrian who was walking along the pavement with his dog. The impact threw him through the hedge and when he was found, he was dead. My colleagues from this ambulance are endeavouring to recover his body as we speak. I'd like you to come to the police station. Mrs. Sanders, I imagine that the most convenient thing is for you to accompany your husband in the patrol car. We will arrange for your car to be collected and taken for forensic examination.'

Both of them still looked shocked. As Sam got up to leave the ambulance he heard Mrs. Sanders say, 'Are you sure? It isn't some tramp who's died in the hedge or something like that?'

'It's not our job to jump to conclusions, ma'am, but the man has multiple fractures and it would have been impossible for him to walk there.'

Sam watched as the paramedics extracted the body from the hedge and lifted the stretcher into the ambulance. Everything at the scene seemed to be under control, so Sam set off with the dog to the address on the collar.

CHAPTER 5

Bad news

Sam took the lead in his left hand and stroked the dog's head.

'What are we going to find when we get you home? Someone should be looking for you by now.' I'm talking to a dog, he thought. Maybe the dog's owner was on his way to the pub, maybe he lives alone? One thing's certain, it's a law-abiding house; I've never had to come here before.

He led the dog around the corner and set off along the road. After a hundred yards he turned up a small track, using his torch to avoid tripping in the potholes. At the end of the lane was a cottage. Sam paused at the gate, a neat latch, a drive at the side leading to a garage with an up and over door, closed at the moment, so it was impossible to know what was inside. The front garden was neat, a few flower beds, looking a bit bedraggled, hardly surprising for the time of year. The lawn was trimmed but by now the grass wouldn't be growing. Sam tried hard to form some sort of picture, looking for feminine touches or signs of children. He'd pretty much given up on that idea when he spotted the side of a trampoline in the back garden. It was covered at the moment but a likely sign of at least one teenage child.

His heart sank. The knock on the door was about to reveal yet another widow, or worse still a child, suddenly having to cope with awful news, or both, maybe. The thought stopped him for a moment. He retreated out of sight and phoned HQ.

'Any chance I could get a WPC over here? I'm about to tell a woman that her husband's been killed. I think there's at least one child in the house and we need the wife to come to the morgue to identify the body. I need some help.'

He hung on for a minute, listening.

'OK, half an hour, I can probably cope for that long. Please be as quick as you can.' He gave them the address, dug a Mars bar out of his pocket, munched his way through half of it, re-wrapped the rest and stuffed it back in his pocket.

He patted the dog's head again and set off slowly down the path. All the curtains were closed but some chinks of light escaped here and there suggesting that someone was in the house. These conversations are never any fun, he thought. Where do I start? Is this your dog, perhaps?

He rang the bell, holding the dog on a short leash so that he would be visible immediately. He patted the animal again; the last thing he needed was an excitable barking dog.

A woman opened the door. Sam's police notebook mind recorded: late thirties, 5,5, blond, looks natural. She was wearing jeans and a loose sweater, no jewellery, carpet slippers. She took one look at Sam, glanced at the dog and said, 'Oh God, I knew something had happened to John.'

'There's been an accident.'

She knelt down and pulled the dog towards her, her fingers working into the fur on the back of the neck. She took the lead from Sam's hand and said, 'Come in.' She unclipped the dog's lead and allowed it to walk past her into the house. Standing to one side, she beckoned Sam forwards into a small hall, closed the door behind her and stepped across the room to open a door on the left.

'Best come in here,' she said.

Sam moved into the room and the woman switched on the light, closed the door behind her and leaned against the wall.

'Is John badly hurt?' she said. 'I had an awful feeling about an hour ago, a feeling that something dreadful had happened. No one phoned, so I thought I was being silly.'

Sam was taken aback; this wasn't how the conversation was supposed to go. He needed to get back onto familiar territory.

'Would you like to sit down?' he said.

She looked him straight in the eye, her brow furrowing and her hand moved involuntarily to her mouth.

'That bad,' she said. 'Is he dead?'

There was no escape, no easy way into this, no coming at it sideways. Sam found himself desperately wanting to play for time, wanting to find some way to soften the blow.

'I'm sorry to sound formal. A man has been killed. When we found him, the dog was with him but he had no identification on him. I don't want to jump to the conclusion that it is your husband, but it does seem likely.'

'Perhaps I will sit down.' She waved at one of the chairs, 'Please,' she said.

Sam sat, trying his best not to show relief at getting the weight off his feet.

'What happened?'

'A car went off the road in the Avenue. Obviously, in the dark, we can't be exactly sure what happened but we found the dog standing over a man lying in the hedge who had obviously been struck by the car. By the time I found him he was dead. An ambulance had already been called, so the paramedics confirmed that. They've taken him to the mortuary in town.'

Sam paused, letting it sink in, waiting for questions,

for tears or some reaction.

There was a long silence.

'I should know what to say,' she said. 'I'm a nurse; it's just that usually it's me saying what you are saying. People always ask; did he suffer? Was he lying there a long time?'

'I'm not a doctor, ma'am, so I'd be guessing. There will have to be a coroner's post-mortem. If my guess is worth anything, I'd say he was probably unconscious the moment the car hit him.'

Another long silence.

'What about the car? There must have been people in it. Are they hurt?'

'No, both of them are very shaken and the driver is under arrest.'

'Under arrest?'

'For suspicion of causing death by dangerous driving. He's down at the station now. That's about all the facts I can give you. I can't say for sure what will happen; it's not an open-and-shut case, the driver said he was swerving to avoid another car. It will all have to be investigated.'

'Doesn't bring John back, does it?'

Sam watched as her face crumbled, then she caught herself.

'I know what happens now,' she said. 'I have to identify the body. I have a teenage daughter. Do I bring her with me? Do you stay here?'

'First we get some reinforcements,' said Sam. 'I've got a policewoman on the way over. I know that doesn't solve anything, but it gives us more options.'

They sat in silence for a few moments.

'Sometimes I have to go the hospital urgently. Probably best if Anna thinks it's that, at least for the moment. How long will your colleague be?'

Sam shook his head. 'Don't know 'til she gets here, but I asked for her to be as quick as possible.'

'Can you phone or something? I'd like to get this done before it catches up with me.'

Sam phoned.

'Should be here in a couple of minutes.'

She got up and opened the curtain a foot. In another minute, a blue light could be seen coming up the lane.

'It has to be tonight, I suppose? If it's not him and he's simply gone to the pub, we'd look a bit silly and someone else ...' Her voice trailed off. 'Someone else would have a terrible night,' she said. 'Better let this lady in.' She got up to go to the door.

Sam hauled himself out of the chair. As he walked to the door, he heard, 'I've got to go the hospital love. The police are giving me a lift, one of them will stay with you. Sorry love, got to rush.'

Sam felt himself being dragged along. He had a moment to share a few words with WPC Andrews and then they were both in the car and heading for the mortuary.

'You might wonder why I'm not in floods of tears,' she said.

'It takes people different ways, I've seen most.'

'I knew something had happened. I had this terrible feeling—dread and confusion all at once. I didn't know where anything was. Can you imagine being lost in your own kitchen? I couldn't find anything, I had to sit down. I felt as though I was on a different planet.' She paused. 'Silly thing to say. I've never been to a different planet, don't suppose you have either. It was like somewhere I'd never been before. Like somewhere I've never even imagined or dreamed before. I had to sit down. Anna was worried about me, she thought I was having a stroke. She even made me a cup of tea.' She laughed nervously for a moment. 'So that's one for the record books. Have you got any children?'

Sam was concentrating on driving, so the question

caught him by surprise.

'No, I'm not married.' Now she'll think I'm some kind of boring loser, he thought. 'I'm not against the idea, just no one has asked me.'

She sighed as he changed gear and eased his way around a bend in the road.

'Sorry, I'm making small talk,' she said. 'you know the man's supposed to do the asking.'

'Well alright, true enough. I tend to meet people in rather unusual circumstances and keep somewhat irregular hours, which gets in the way of a social life.'

'Am I daft to think that funny turn was something to do with John?'

Sam glanced at her and then back to the road, trying to think what to say. Not wanting to cause upset he decided to be neutral.

'I'm not the person to ask. I've heard all sorts of things over the years but it's hard to prove one way or the other.'

'It wouldn't stand up in court, you mean? I was proceeding down the high street when I had this premonition, your Honour. That sort of thing.'

'That's um ...'

'A bit cruel? It's a cruel night ... Do you think he was lying there long? You know, lying there dying and not able to do anything about it. Was he trying to tell me something? I could have been there in no time if I'd known.'

'It's better not to think about things like that. We have to be sure it's John before anything else.'

'It will be, I'm sure of that.' As she said it, he could hear the light go out of her voice and silence descended on them for the last few miles.

Morgues are never friendly places; people don't go there unless they have to and this one was no different. They made their way through security and down a bland characterless corridor, with a pair of rubber slam doors at the end.

It took a moment for the attendant to pull the body out of the chiller and another second to uncover his face.

Sam watched as she stretched out her hand and smoothed the hair away from the forehead.

'Goodbye, love,' she whispered.

She cried most of the way back. A few miles from home, WPC Andrews phoned, partly to check on progress but also to say that the daughter was becoming anxious because her father had not come home.

'We'll be five minutes,' said Sam, then turning to the woman next to him, 'there's a box of tissues in the glove compartment.'

'Thanks. You must have had this happen before.'

'Once or twice.'

'What am I going to tell her?'

'Do you want me to talk to her?'

'What good would that do? You'll have to go eventually and then there's just us.'

'I'm sorry.'

She pulled a tissue out of the box and dabbed her eyes.

'I'm going to look bloody awful whatever I do. I've done this you know, talked to relatives about death, but not to my own daughter.'

'Better she should hear it from someone who knows how to do it.'

'Do they train you to produce these platitudes or is it a natural talent?'

Sam took a quick look at her face; there was a hint of a fierce smile and some fire back in her eyes. He didn't say another word until they were pulling into the lane.

'Do you want me to be with you?'

'Is that OK? It might be best if you can tell her what

happened but be ready for fireworks, I've no idea how she'll react.'

Well, she was right about that—tears, moaning and a couple of punches; it was all a blur by the time she was exhausted and Sam finally managed to leave. Halfway home he remembered the other half of the chocolate bar, thought about it for a moment and decided sleep was a better idea.

CHAPTER 6

Widows in a line

Sticking pins in maps is old-fashioned. These days it's all done with software and clever gizmos but old-fashioned works. Technology is great, when it's second nature, but not if you have to think about the details; it takes your mind off the real problem. You don't have to think about the pins, just where they are and the patterns they make.

Sam Diglis had a big map; it covered half the wall in what an estate agent would have called his living room. As each new case came along it got its own pin. When the case was completed, the pin came out and the papers were filed away.

Some of the pins had coloured string attached, connecting them to other pins; a private code that represented how sure Sam was about the link. A series of burglaries with what looked like the same Modus Operandi might get a dark string. Relatives of a subject under investigation would be green string. Some of the string did not connect to other pins at all, it might stretch across to pictures or notes stuck on the rest of the wall. It was a kind of private code. It made sense to Sam and if no one else could get it, well all the better.

Most days the only meal that Sam could be sure of eating at home was breakfast. He could have eaten with his back to the map but what would be the point? Sam liked looking at the pins and strings each day; it helped him focus. He'd stare at the map, letting the patterns emerge in his mind and allowing himself a frisson of annoyance at the lone pins with no connections.

This was one of those days when his mind was in neutral. A piece of toast was half way to his mouth when he realised something very odd about the tragic events of the last few months.

'A straight line, a bloody straight line, why the hell would that be?'

He carefully put the toast back on his plate and walked around the table to the map. First, he examined each pin very carefully, making sure that they were in the right place. He moved closer to the wall and sighted along the line of the pins. There was no doubt about it, they were in a dead straight line. Not evenly spaced but straight all the same. He rummaged briefly in a drawer and pulled out a steel rule. He carefully measured the distances between the pins and noted them on a blank page in his notebook. He stared at the numbers for a while then shrugged, put the notebook back in his jacket and returned to the toast. He took a swig of coffee and said in a rasping voice, 'Detective Diglis, is it quite impossible to get me a hot cup of tea?' He laughed. 'Time. That is the crucial ingredient. The time it takes from the teapot to the cup, time when you should be concentrating on the task in hand, namely getting me my tea.' He laughed again and gave up imitating his old boss's voice. 'Fitz sure was a mean old bastard.'

He finished the toast and drank the rest of the cold tea, picked up his jacket, started for the door and then stopped.

'I told you time was the crucial ingredient,' he said in the same rasping voice. He wrote the date and time of the jumble sale on a clean page. After a moment he added dates and times for the cattle stampede and the car crash. It took a few minutes with a calculator and a lot of muttering under his breath before he had the interval between the events in minutes. He glanced at the measurements from the map and did some more calculations.

He frowned, wrote some numbers down and did the calculation again. 'Bloody Hell, they are connected by time.' He sat back in the chair and stared at the map on the wall.

'Makes no sense at all. All three events were crazy but what could make crazy events happen in sequence on a straight line? I'm bloody glad I'm not trying to explain that one to Fitz. Job for the back burner that one,' he said and set off out of the house.

Each of the events in question had a widow attached and each of the widows had a tendency to phone Sam about once a week. He kept telling himself this was entirely understandable; each of the three women were enveloped in a massive tragedy, each would have to cope with an inquest and were desperate for information to help them make sense of what had happened. Sam's problem was that he didn't have much to go on. The Coroner's Office worked at a glacial pace and each case was entirely different.

The jumble sale had become complicated once the CID had agreed the identification of the young man and linked him up with a string of fraud and deception cases. They'd worked out that him running away was the start of the problem but why did he run? Someone in a back office had become convinced that this was a "promising line of enquiry." He must have seen a former accomplice or someone who frightened him and that made him run. If they could identify that person then they might unlock a heap of unsolved crimes.

'Yeah,' thought Sam when they told him, 'and delay the inquest 'til kingdom come.'

The delay just gave Dwayne's mum more time to brood. Why was Dwayne sitting on the vicar's knee? Was the vicar up to something? Then she started asking every mother in the village if they had any suspicions that the vicar was a paedophile. Thankfully, the vicar's wife had the sense not to react but it didn't help.

The cattle stampede should have been easy but once she had her wits back Ellen wanted to know if there was something the matter with the cows. Was it a kind of mad cow disease? The local vet was out of his depth so the boffins at the agricultural college were dragged in, except they didn't have a big enough freezer. In the end they'd had to hire a refrigerated lorry that was now parked behind the college as they worked their way through slices of brain and who knows what in biochemical tests. That just made it another inquest that was disappearing into the middle distance.

Finally, the car crash. Sam had taken statements from the driver and his passenger and they were both sure that he'd swerved to avoid a black car coming the other way. The driver of the vehicle that he'd been overtaking hadn't seen another car but it was getting dark and maybe the car didn't have its lights on. Sam had gone over the statements of both drivers several times and concluded that they'd get nowhere putting any of the witnesses on the stand. Any decent lawyer could conjure up a reasonable doubt. Was there a record of the black car somewhere?

An hour of looking at the map and checking databases tracked down every camera on every road that could lead to the Avenue. As he listed them and placed them on the map, it soon became obvious that the village was surrounded by cameras. Sam tried to imagine how long it would take to search all the footage. Maybe someone in Traffic could help. That left the stretches of road with no cameras and all the places a car could come from nearer the scene; if a car came from somewhere local and never appeared on any cameras it had still to be somewhere local.

Sam went back to his notes. What did they really know about the car? Reading the witness statements, it could have been anything—a truck even, or maybe a van. On reflection probably not a truck, Sam thought. It was going too fast but something like a Transit van or that sort of thing could get a decent turn of speed.

He read the statements given to other officers and his brows wrinkled. He did another Fitz impression.

'Wipe that frown off your face boy. Engage the brain not the eyebrows.

'They're talking about it almost as if they'd seen a ghost,' he said out loud to himself.

The thought haunted him all day. Three bizarre events, all in a line, each set off by something. A young man who suddenly runs for his life and no one knows what he's seen. A driver who swerves to miss something that no one else can see. Well, something that no one outside of his car can see or was the wife just backing him up? Cows spooked by something no one saw. Did they all see a ghost?

'Add all that up and where does it get me?' thought Sam. Three widows all phoning me and wanting me to tell them what happened. I'm going to have to do better than a ghost story.

CHAPTER 7

The Pathologist

It took a couple of weeks to get an appointment with the pathologist and despite as much preparation as he could think of Sam still approached the conversation with some trepidation.

'If you can take me through exactly what happened to the poor man, I'd be very grateful. I have to piece it together with the other information that's coming in,' that's what Sam had said on the phone to the pathologist. He had not said, 'I've met the widow several times and she's desperate to know because she had some sort of premonition around the time of the accident and it's playing on her mind.'

They met in the doctor's office, not as intimidating as the mortuary but still lined with books and odd specimens in jars that might phase less hardy souls. Sam's worry was not the pieces of dead people sitting in jars, more that he hoped he would understand what was said. Looking like an idiot while wearing a uniform is no fun.

Doctor Pearson spread a rough map on the desk in front of him and began speaking. He had a somewhat formal style, as though he were dictating a report or speaking in court.

'John Roberts was walking north along the Avenue. There are four lanes on the roadway, separated by white lines. There is no central reservation. It is within a forty miles an hour zone. The Maserati driven by Mr Sanders was travelling in the same direction coming up behind him. It moved out, probably using the second and third lane, as it overtook a car in lane one. You will note that I am making the assumption that it at least partly ventured into lane three. I do this in order to make some sense of its later movements. Yes?'

'I thought the same, though Mr Sander's statement said he stayed in lane two.'

'Well, he would say that wouldn't he.'

Sam nodded and the doctor went on.

'The Maserati is a fast car; if Mr Sanders put his foot down to overtake he'd probably give the car on the inside a wide berth. Be that as it may, at some point he swerved back across to the northbound lanes and lost control. He came back at an angle, crossed both northbound lanes and hit the curb. Was it you who photographed the mark on the curb?'

'Yes, but I think the traffic people took some more pictures.'

'No matter, he hit the curb, bounced up, flew through the air and hit the tree. At that point we know he was over two feet off the ground. The mark on the tree matches with the dent in the bumper.'

'Have you got that from the forensics?' asked Sam.

'Yes, and some more information that I will come to. The impact made a big dent in the tree. The car bounced back and spun in mid air so that it was then travelling along, above the pavement towards where Mr Roberts was walking. The car was spinning around in mid air, so with the tyres off the ground there would be no friction so it probably spun quite fast.'

He rummaged in a drawer and pulled out a model car, ran it across the map and turned it in mid air.

'So the Maserati was spinning anti-clockwise and as it came around to the point where it was facing backwards, the driver's side back wing hit Mr Roberts and knocked him across the pavement and through the hedge. The car carried on spinning, through a complete rotation and a little more. It eventually landed sideways across the road, front end on the curb and the rear jutting out into the road. A dirt mark on the road shows exactly where it landed and the car slid sideways another yard before finally coming to rest. Fibres from Mr Roberts' clothes have been found embedded in the driver's side wing.'

'Bloody hell,' said Sam, 'so it hit him very hard?'

'Exactly. When it hit him, the side of the car was going north and swiping sideways simultaneously. I think we can assume that Mr Roberts would have known nothing about it. I've done some work on that, out of curiosity. Let's say the car was going at 40mph, the speed limit, though it was probably quicker because he was overtaking. At that speed a car travels around 60 feet in a second, so the time from the bang against the tree to the impact with Mr Roberts is about three-tenths of a second. Keep in mind that some of those three-tenths are used up by the sound travelling to him and his ear telling his brain. The fastest sprinters take almost one and a half tenths to move at all after the gun and they know which way to go. Even if he had very fast reflexes and even if he guessed which way to jump, he would have had no way of avoiding something as big as a car.'

'Would he have been knocked out immediately?'

'Coming to that, coming to that.' The doctor put the car down.

'So now we come to the injuries. It's hard to be precise about the first point of impact as the car was still in the air and so we can only speculate as to the exact height. The driver of the car that was being overtaken thought it got up about four feet, probably an exaggeration, and he would have had a less than good view after the impact with the tree. We know from the debris on the road that there must have been a cloud of debris - road dirt from the underside of the car and general mess out of the hedge. The car must have hit Mr Roberts around his middle. What we do know is that he had a smashed pelvis, a broken femur, thigh bone to you, and numerous broken ribs. I think your report mentioned the ribs, very observant of you.'

'I was trying to see if he was breathing. When I put my hand on his chest I could feel it cave in.'

'Quite right, quite right. At that point I'd say his injuries were barely survivable. If you had been there immediately it is possible that breathing for him would have helped but the internal bleeding from the injuries would have killed him in a few minutes.'

'It's OK, Doc, I'm not feeling guilty that I could have saved him.'

'Yes, well, one never knows. Anyway, there's more. His ribs were smashed but the impact also tore his lung in three places. The lung is like a massive sponge but weaving between all the air sacs are blood vessels. They run very close to the air sacs so that oxygen can diffuse across into the blood; oxygen comes in and carbon dioxide goes out. Tear the lung apart and blood will leak out and if you try to blow air in it will leak as well. Of course, he still had one lung that was in one piece but he wouldn't have been able to breathe himself. The chest wall was so smashed up that any effort from his respiratory muscles and diaphragm would have just made it flap about. No air would have gone in. He couldn't have shouted either so unless one of the witnesses had seen him go into the hedge, there was no way they'd have known he was there.' He paused for a second.

'This isn't too gruesome for you?'

'No, Doc, you carry on,' said Sam, thinking he might not tell Mr Roberts' wife the whole thing.

'Well, in a way it was probably better that no one found him because they'd have got nowhere. The impact on his chest tore a hole in his heart so his few remaining heartbeats would have filled his chest with blood, if his heart was still beating. The shock of the injury probably stopped it anyway.'

'It really smashed him up.'

'You could say that, though no doubt the court will require details. His right arm was broken and I suspect that happened before his head hit the car. His body must have wrapped itself around the car so his head would have been the last to hit. It broke his skull in several places and ripped his brain apart.'

'Would he have felt anything?'

'No.'

'Can you be sure of that?' said Sam, convinced that this would be what mattered most to Maria Roberts and her daughter.

'As I've said, he might possibly have heard the bang as the car hit the tree. After that you have to remember that when an object is spinning around the ends move faster than the middle, so the part that hit him was probably travelling at about 70mph. At that speed it covers about a hundred feet in a second. It must have done all the damage in about one or two feet. That would take about a fiftieth of a second from the first touch to breaking almost every bone in his body. The fastest nerves in the body conduct impulses at one hundred and twenty metres per second. In a fiftieth of a second a nerve impulse might manage to travel the distance from the foot to the brain. One impulse getting to the brain isn't the same as feeling anything. To turn an impulse into thought many other cells must connect and process the information. There wasn't time for that before his brain was in pieces. There is no way that Mr. Roberts knew what hit him or even felt anything. His brain must have been torn apart and not working before any sensation could have reached it from any part of his body.'

'So he died instantly.'

'Let's not get into a philosophical discussion about

how long an instant is. He certainly died without knowing anything about it. A good deal faster than if he'd had a heart attack or a stroke.'

CHAPTER 8

Maria Roberts

Sam spent the morning doing routine work but in the back of his mind was what to do about Maria Roberts. Should he call her and invite her to the station to pass on what he had from the pathologist or should he call at her house? The station was on safe ground but it might make it seem too formal. There was no requirement on him to say anything; the coroner's inquest would be bound to tell her everything she needed to know. On the other hand, that was not going to happen for months. The traffic people and the automotive engineers were still working on finding the black car and trying to figure out the precise dynamics of the crash. Could they work backwards from the damage to know how fast the car was travelling? If they could prove that the car was speeding then they had a solid case and the black car mattered less; breaking the speed limit was against the law. If they couldn't do that then the black vehicle was crucial if they wanted to remove all reasonable doubt.

He'd have to go to her house but the next question was when. Maybe during the day was best, less chance of the daughter being home, so at least Maria would have time to get over any upset. Of course she might be working, but nurses do funny shifts. What if she'd been doing nights? What time would she get up? About now, he thought, and closed up the station and drove down to the lane.

In daylight the house looked charming, or maybe it was simply that Sam was not approaching the door with no idea what he might encounter. This time the uncertainty and the tears were out of the way and when Sam arrived Maria made tea. Sam tried to watch her face and body language without seeming to stare. Were there signs of strain, had she been crying too much? It was hard to tell. Whatever was going on in her mind she was showing a brave face to the world.

Sam worked his way through what the pathologist had told him, tentatively at first but getting into his stride as she seemed to be able to cope.

'I can't claim to be on top of all the technical stuff but the important thing is that between the car hitting the tree and hitting your husband, there was less than half a second. Not enough time for anything to register. Another fraction of a second after that his heart was torn apart and his brain was in three pieces. It sounds brutal but what it adds up to is that he could not possibly have known anything about it.'

Maria sat quietly for a long time but eventually she said, 'I told you before, I'm a nurse. I'd probably understand all that medical stuff better than you. Were you supposed to tell me all that?'

'I'm not sure. I can't see that it does any harm, you'll hear it all at the inquest.'

'When will that be?'

'That's partly why I told you now, it may be months.'

'Why?'

'They have to decide whether to charge the driver. That means they have to put all the evidence together, analysis of the car, trying to find the black car he says he saw, all that stuff and then they have to try to persuade the Crown Prosecution Service. If they prosecute, then to put it simply the court case becomes the inquest. If the CPS doesn't take the case then we have the inquest with the coroner. It's going to take some time.'

She looked straight at him and raised her eyebrows.

'Months rather than weeks,' said Sam.

'I don't understand why it's so difficult. He flew off the road, hit a tree and killed my husband. That has to be dangerous driving.'

'This is where I might begin to regret coming here.'

She waved her arms, as though she were scrubbing a blackboard.

'No, no, don't fret, I'm not going to tell anyone, this is off the record.'

'You could have the conversation with the CPS,' said Sam, 'but they won't talk to you until they've made up their mind. You could find all this on the internet, so don't blame me. Right?'

'Right, but will we have to wait that long for the funeral?'

'No. Once the police and the coroner have all the evidence they need then they'll release John's body. What takes the time is the police processing what they have. Not just the post-mortem, there's also evidence from the car, the road and everything else. They give that to the CPS who have to decide whether to prosecute. The CPS apply two tests. First test—is there a better than even chance of a successful prosecution? Second test—is it in the public interest to bring the case to court? They apply the tests in that order so if they don't think they'll win, then they won't prosecute, even if it might be in the public interest. Personally I'd do it the other way around but I didn't make the rules.'

Sam watched her face, looking for some reaction but didn't see anything so he went on.

'If the driver says he swerved to avoid someone else, then a good lawyer stands a fair chance of convincing a jury that it was the other car's fault. After that, it's up to us to find that other car. It's hard to prove the negative. We may not find the other car but that doesn't prove it doesn't exist. Not beyond all reasonable doubt and that's the standard of proof for a criminal case.'

'And if you do find the car?'

'Well, then we have to see what the other driver says. If he says he was on the correct side of the road going at a reasonable speed and this sports coupé came charging at him, then, if he or she seems like a credible witness then I guess the CPS would prosecute.'

He could see her eyes narrow.

'Do you think that Mr. Sanders was smart enough to make up something like that on the spur of the moment? Did he have a legal background? Would he know that was a good excuse?'

'It's not for me to say.'

'Off the record.'

Sam looked at her carefully for a moment; she leant forward in the chair and the intensity of her gaze was almost disturbing.

'He'd seen something, and his wife had, something that shocked them.' Sam stopped for a moment to clear his memory. 'I'm not an expert on body language but it wasn't just that they'd almost wrapped themselves around a tree, and at that stage, I don't think they'd even seen your husband, they both looked as though they'd seen a ghost. They'd seen something that scared the hell out of them. I don't think they were in any fit state to make up clever stories.'

'So if you don't find the black car, or van, then you're looking for a ghost.'

'I didn't say that.'

'Well, you sort of did,' said Maria. 'OK, I know there's no such thing as ghosts and even if there are I've never heard of ghost trucks, but maybe it was some sort of natural phenomenon. What was the weather like? They didn't see a small whirlwind or something or some sort of shadow from a tree?'

'Who knows? It doesn't help. Anything like that

isn't going to get very far with the CPS or a jury. That's the thing, Maria, that's what I'm trying to explain. You have to prepare yourself for the possibility that the CPS will do nothing and Sanders will get off.'

Her face changed but not in the way Sam expected. She half smiled, a sort of wry grin.

'You're talking like a policeman, Sam. Is it OK to call you Sam?' She glanced at him. 'I just want to know what happened to John, but locking someone up doesn't bring him back. I don't mind you wanting to prosecute someone but you don't have to do that for me. I want to know what happened. That's all.'

CHAPTER 9

Detecting

Sam phoned 'The Detectives' as Mrs Adams, Dwayne's mother, had called them.

'Anything more on the jumble sale massacre?'

'We've talked to everyone who was there, as far as we can tell.'

'Any leads?'

'It's complicated. About your young man, it's hard to say; we have his name and a thick file. He was a smart lad; most of the record is suspicions rather than verdicts. We have a whole heap of possible associations with other dubious characters but something doesn't quite add up.'

'What?'

'All his form is in the antique business but none of his likely associates were at the sale. There are some "people of interest", as you might say, who were there but none of them have any link to the antiques trade. Either our lad was branching out into new fields or we're missing something. One way or another it doesn't add up. On the other hand, the good news is that some of the locals are ringing bells; any chance you could come over and see if we can fill in the blanks?'

Sam's curiosity was aroused.

'Could you send me a list of who you might be interested in and I'll see what I can bring.'

Half an hour later Sam had the list on his desk and a rapid read raised enough curiosity to get him into the car.

He phoned ahead and had a quick word with Colin.

'Hello, my old mate, how's tricks? I'm coming over to see two of your young men, Terry Ashton and Rick Small, what's the word on them?'

'Smart young lads.'

'Bit full of themselves, you mean?'

'Never said a word.'

'OK to park in the usual place?'

'No problem. Drop in when you're done, I'm here for hours yet.'

By the time he arrived they had most of the information on a wall.

'This car is the object of interest,' said Terry. 'It's been seen in the company of another vehicle we've been keeping tabs on. Do you know anything about the owner, a Mr Garside?'

'He's a farmer, operates about eight miles away from the village.'

'Any previous, to your knowledge?'

'You've run him through all the databases?'

'Yeah, yeah, course we have, but you know … What about local knowledge?'

'He's a hard up farmer. His place is a bit too small for modern farming, looked a tad run down last time I was there. I'd expect him to sell up before long. What have you connected him with?'

Sam walked over to the wall, pointing at aerial shots of the farm.

'This is off Google, right? I reckon it's a bit out of date, some of the buildings don't look quite right and those are summer crops.'

'Yeah, well we just wanted the general layout.'

'You've got that alright. It's very out of the way, long lane up to it, they'd see you coming if you were going to raid it.'

'Not ready for that.'

'So what are you after?'

Small spoke next, with a slight shrug of the shoulders and what Sam thought was defensive body language.

'The bloke we were watching is a long time no good and he's made a pile of money recently. He's into something new but we don't know what and we sure as hell don't know what your farmer has to do with it.'

'Maybe it's just a coincidence.'

This time Ashton spoke.

'No, we caught his car in our sights twice. Once might be chance but not twice. There's a connection there, but we don't know what.'

'When you say a pile of money, any idea how much?'

'We haven't got at his bank account or anything but we think we're talking hundreds of thousands.'

Sam strolled around the wallboard again, looking more closely at the farm buildings.

'Were you thinking of some sort of surveillance?'

'What do you reckon?'

'Not easy. I could pop down there for a chat and say there's been some rustling or something. He's got some livestock so he wouldn't suspect. I could have a look around. It'd be too tricky to do something like leave a camera in the hedge.'

'What's the bloke like?'

'Bit of a loner, always looks a bit scruffy. That's why I figure he's not doing too well. He's not paranoid or anything, he won't come at you with a shot gun, well, not unless he's changed a bit.'

Sam stopped for a moment, looked at the two detectives and back at the pictures of the farm.

'Know what I reckon? Want to hear a wild guess?'

'Go on then.'

'Smuggling, cigarettes, that's what I think. Perfect set up. Someone nicks a lorry off a motorway at night or something like that, and well before dawn it's parked in one of those barns. The buildings are certainly big enough, you could hide a truck there no problem; it could sit there out of sight for as long as you like. Empty it out when you feel like it, take the stuff out in little white vans; probably don't even need to do that at night. Put some logo on the side that looks like farm delivery, feedstuff, fertiliser, you name it. They could even have a few bags of genuine farm stuff in the back to fool a quick inspection. OK, it's a long lane and a small farm but there's trucks up and down often enough that a few more won't be noticed.'

Sam glanced again at the two men.

'What's the duty and tax on a container load of fags? A million or so?'

'We did think of that.'

Sam grinned, 'Yeah of course you did, only trouble is you'd have to share the collar with the excise boys, bit less glory to go round.'

'Yeah, yeah,' said Ashton. 'Any chance you could have a sniff around?'

'I can do better than that.'

'Meaning?'

'There's traffic cameras on that road, one about two miles south, another a bit further going north but it's got to be a reasonable shot. Worth a look.'

'Probably not switched on.'

Sam grinned, 'Wrong there, both of them are working fine.'

'Did they get you speeding?'

Sam shook his head.

'O ye of little faith. They've been part of another investigation, which I happen to be aware of, ongoing as we speak.' He watched their faces and grinned again.

'There was a bad crash on my patch, we've been looking for a particular vehicle, nothing very brilliant lads, but the boys in traffic might let you see their home movies. Now while I'm here, have you found anything on our young antiques trader? Why did he take off like the hounds of hell were after him?'

They both shrugged, and Ashton said, 'Honestly Sam, we don't have a clue. The way he ran, or at least what the witnesses say, we thought there must have been a major figure he was scared of, or a hit man maybe. If anyone at that sale was an important crook in that trade they've kept it bloody quiet.'

Small interrupted.

'You've read all the statements, I guess? Someone said he looked like he'd seen a ghost, maybe he thought he recognised someone, but who knows?'

'Maybe he did see a ghost.'

'Yeah maybe, Sam, but there's no way you can do a ghost for upsetting the neighbours.'

Sam gathered up his papers and closed his briefcase.

'Keep me posted. I'll do what I said and have a wander up there, look for tyre tracks and the like.'

CHAPTER 10

Walking the line

If there was something that connected the three tragedies then there might be a clue somewhere along the line. Sam spent a few hours studying the map and more time on the internet before deciding that the only thing to do was walk the line, or, more accurately, ride the line on his cross country motorcycle. He spent some more time transferring the line to a one inch Ordinance Survey map and decided the best place to start would be from the site of the jumble sale.

Behind the church was a large field that was used as a cricket pitch in the summer. Now it was just a broad green featureless expanse. It hardly looked like a source of trouble. Sam took the lane that ran alongside the field and made a new start the other side. A small cottage was almost exactly on the line. The owner was well known, if only because he had given up cursing about cricket balls through his greenhouse and now offered a prize for anyone who could hit a six that big. His reasoning, as he would explain at length to anyone who bought him a pint, was that if they were aiming at it, they would probably miss. He also hoped that thinking about the reward might tempt batsmen into having a go at it when the ball was not quite right and hence they would get out. He rather hoped that this would apply to the opposition more than the local side. The locals, he thought, might well have discovered that he had invested in armoured glass for the roof.

He might have an evil imagination, thought Sam, but I know for sure that he was away with his folks in the USA for at least a couple of weeks before the jumble sale, so there was no way the mysterious "something" that wrecked the jumble sale and caused the other catastrophes could have been some new trick he was up to. As he rolled past the cottage Sam almost laughed at himself. It was important to keep an open mind but the guy from the cottage was not an invisible death ray kind of person; if he were up to something the whole world would know.

Behind the cottage was woodland, rolling uphill almost to the top of the ridge. Sam took a bearing before venturing into the trees; the line went almost to the top of the hill. It crested the ridge to one side of the summit at an area where there was a hump. It had always been thought to be an old burial mound. No one in living memory anyway had opened it up. He'd had a complaint once that someone was prowling around it with a metal detector but by the time he'd got up there they'd gone, and he heard no more about it. That was the thing in the country, you had to be seen to respond and everything was OK, no one ever asked about the final outcome. Mostly it was a few lines in the logbook and nothing more. That at least meant that if anything similar came up there was a date and time to refer back to.

Before he set out Sam had decided that the motorbike would be better than walking, that way, if nothing turned up, he could at least carry on down the other side of the ridge. Sam rode into the trees trying to follow a compass bearing, not a simple matter when a large tree is in your path. Fortunately, this was mature woodland so the shade from the big trees had stopped any scrub from growing. He made steady progress uphill. The big problem was knowing what he was looking for.

There were no signs of disturbance, the moss was growing on the right side of the trees, there were no split trunks, no fallen branches, just a silent, peaceful, woodland. Sam stopped from time to time to cut the sound of his engine and listen to the birds. Everything sounded and looked normal.

After a while the trees thinned out and he could see the barrow against the sky. At least he'd kept to the right line.

When he reached the ancient mound he stopped, took a moment to get the bike on its stand and walked around the mound.

If you're a police officer, looking for something that seems out of place is second nature but what is normal in a five-thousand-year-old mound? The grass was long with some bracken amongst it. There were no signs of footsteps or disturbance. He climbed to the top of the mound and looked down. Heading onwards, in line with his previous track, there was a faint suggestion that the grass had parted, probably a wind effect but out of curiosity he walked down the line. At the bottom of the mound he found the remains of four dead rabbits, what looked like two adults and two juveniles. They had been dead some while, the fur was matted and the muscles and interior had rotted but it seemed strange that no other scavenger had made off with the free meat. Did these luckless rabbits have some part in the mystery?

There was nothing else so he remounted the motorbike and carefully picked his way down the hill. The ride was made a little easier by the presence of what seemed like a sheep track, or maybe it was sightseers who had flattened the grass walking up to the mound. One thing was for sure, the marks in the grass were right on his compass bearing. When he was two-thirds of the way down the hill he stopped again, parked the bike and used his binoculars to study the ground in front of him. The next field was stubble that had once been a crop of maize. He spent some time scanning across the field, trying to see any change in pattern that fitted the line he was following. After five minutes he had convinced himself that there was a track across the field. There was a slight change in the soil colour, a few stones that looked as though they were in a line and maybe a hint that the stalks of the cut plants were thinner. On the far side of the field, in line with his bearing, was a gate.

So, the path is a path, he thought. A straight line from the gate. He focused the binoculars and for a second he was surprised. The gate was hung from a huge stone, maybe six feet high, set in the hedge. Handy, he thought. A built-in gatepost but what was a huge rock doing there?

He drove down, across the field, parking by the gate to have a close up look at the stone. The gate hinges looked antiquated; two big hooks hammered into the rock. They looked as though they must be hundreds of years old but the stone was older than that. He stood back and looked at the edifice. Half of it was covered by the hedge that had grown round it but there was no mistaking the regular shape. It had four sides that had obviously been chiselled by ancient tools so that each face was flat. It looked like a tall narrow obelisk, though without the traditional pointed top; it was about two feet square at the base and rising to about a foot squared near the top. The last six inches had been cut away to make a smaller stubby pyramid. A bit like the Washington monument or Cleopatra's needle only without the writing and much shorter. Whoever had hung the gate had done a clever job of fashioning hinges that allowed for the taper on the stone.

He took the bike through the gate and parked it in the little road on the other side. That gave him a chance to have a longer look at the stone and take a compass bearing. The stone was on a dead line with the barrow on the ridge of the hill.

'I bet the same people made both,' he muttered. He was still marking the gate on the map when his phone rang. He listened for a moment.

'Dwayne's mother, yes?' He thought for a moment, trying to remember if he owed her a call. 'I can be back at the station in half an hour if that's any help?' He nodded as he listened and a moment later was back on the motorbike heading down the lane.

CHAPTER 11

Dwayne's mother

Dwayne's mother, Mrs Adams, was a small, fussy woman who often seemed slightly distracted, as though she had one too many things to do and something else on her mind that she couldn't quite remember. Conversations with her had a tendency to take odd turns as different ideas flitted through her brain; almost like a computer with too small a memory, never able to hold quite enough information.

'Those detectives, have they found anything?'

'You'd have to ask them. Sorry, Mrs Adams, I don't want to seem like I'm giving you the brush off but they don't tell me everything they are doing. You'll have to talk to them.'

'But they won't tell me anything.'

'What did you ask them?'

'About the vicar, you know, did they know anything about him, was he one of those?'

'I'm not sure I know what you mean, Mrs. Adams.'

'Well, Dwayne was sitting on his knee … He's never done that before.'

'So why do you think it's suspicious?'

'Well, I mean, it must be mustn't it? Do they know about any others? That's what they won't tell me.'

'I'm sorry, Mrs Adams, you're confusing me. You just said he's never done it before.'

There was a long pause and Sam could see confusion running across her face.

'No, I meant the vicar, he's the one I was suspicious about.'

Sam stopped, replaying the conversation in his mind.

'You meant that Dwayne doesn't usually sit on anyone's knee?'

'Yes, he runs around all the time.'

'And you think the vicar might be a paedophile. Did you tell the detectives that?'

'I thought they'd find out.'

Sam took a deep breath.

'Apart from Dwayne sitting on his knee did you have any other suspicions about the vicar?'

'I hardly knew him.'

'Do you go to church?'

'Oh yes.'

'Which church do you go to?'

'That one. The one he's at.' She stopped, her hand flying to her mouth, 'Um, I mean, was at.'

'Do you go every Sunday?'

'Oh no, haven't got the time.'

'When do you go?'

'At Christmas, like everyone does.'

Sam took another deep breath.

'Mrs Adams, normally I wouldn't say anything like this. Usually I would write a note of what you said and leave it at that but I do know that you've been asking the same questions around the village. You do realise that you could be making a very serious allegation about Mr Prentice. If I take you seriously then I will have to notify other authorities, a proper investigation will have to be done and at the moment everyone in the village is very upset because four people died on what was supposed to be a pleasant day raising money for the church.'

'I didn't like to bother you. I thought those other detectives would find out, it's not for me to tell tales is it?'

She stopped and burst into tears. Sam reached for

the box of tissues he kept in his desk drawer; she wasn't the first person to cry in his office and she probably wouldn't be the last.

'I was so relieved to see our Dwayne after he ran off and he looked happy sitting on the vicar's knee. He was holding his collar and then it all exploded. I can't get the picture out of my mind, Dwayne smiling and holding the vicar's neck.'

She dabbed her eyes some more so Sam waited for her to settle.

'I know it's a terrible memory but how long was it? How long was he sitting there?'

'I don't know, I wasn't in the tent. Mrs Prentice came and found me.'

'Yes, but how long was it between when you walked into the tent and the explosion happened?'

'No time at all. I came in, saw Dwayne and …'

She was engulfed in tears again.

'So, no time at all really.'

'No,' she said, 'no time at all.'

Sam pulled over the waste bin and waited while two more tissues dropped into it.

She looked up suddenly, clutching the tissue between two hands and almost tearing it in her agitation.

'Are they suspecting me?'

'Suspecting you?'

'For letting Dwayne run off?'

Sam tried to put himself in her shoes. She was bound to feel guilty. Dwayne had run off, though "off" in this case amounted to about ten yards, and around one corner between two stalls, hardly a major excursion.

'Does it prey on your mind?'

'But why did he run to the vicar?'

'Did he run to the vicar? I thought he was just running, and the vicar caught him. A six year old dashing about among the stalls could get into trouble; I think all Mr Prentice did was catch him.'

Frowns and confusion followed each other across her face.

'He wasn't running away from me.'

'Why do you say that?'

Between more sobs she said, 'I was buying sweets for them, for Dwayne and our Jeremy. Usually he'd be waiting and trying to grab them but he was looking at another stall and then Jeremy yelled something, I don't know what. I thought I must have got the wrong sweets; sometimes they get very picky. I was looking at the sweets and counting the change and telling Jeremy to be quiet and then he started crying and next thing I knew, I saw the back of Dwayne running around the corner of the next stall.'

'What was Jeremy yelling about? Had Dwayne poked him or something?'

More dabbing of eyes followed until eventually, 'No, I don't know what it was. I shouted at Dwayne to come back and I started to go after him but Jeremy grabbed my leg and almost tripped me up. I had to pay attention to him, I don't know what it was.'

Sam thought for a moment, the germ of a new idea creeping into his head.

'What I think you are saying is that something upset both boys, yet this happened while they were waiting for sweets. Odd isn't it, don't you think?' He looked up, meeting her eyes. 'They weren't fighting about the sweets, or fighting about anything else but something suddenly made both of them upset. Has that happened before, do they do that often?'

'Like kicking off and being wicked?'

'No, I mean being scared out of their minds by something that isn't real. Remember what Joyce Prentice said, he ran up yelling about a "bogeyman". Why would he say that? Did Jeremy see a bogeyman?'

Her brows knitted into a ferocious frown. Now I've done it, thought Sam, she's going to explode or tell everyone I'm barmy.

'I've never asked him.'

'Does he talk about that day?'

'No, 'cos I cry. Arthur won't talk about it either, same thing, like here, I'm buying that many tissues. You'd have to ask him, I couldn't.'

'Did the boys know stories with a bogeyman in them?'

There was a long silence until she said, 'It's Arthur's mum, she tells them the bogeyman will get them if they don't go to sleep. We've told her not to, it's daft. Why frighten them? But we have to have her babysit sometimes. She used to say the same to Arthur when he was little.' She grabbed another tissue. 'Don't ask her about it, she'd be awful upset.'

'Don't ask who?' said Sam, trying to keep up.

'Arthur… Jeremy… Arthur's mum. Don't not for now anyway.'

'But why would the boys think there was a bogeyman at the jumble sale?'

Sam got no further. Many tears and tissues were used before Mrs Adams was in a fit state to go home. Sam took her back in the car. As he dropped her off, he said, 'Don't let it upset you, Mrs Adams, you've been very helpful. It gives me something else to work on. I think Dwayne was running away from something, not running to the vicar. We have to try to find out what might have frightened him. If the other detectives come up with anything I'll let you know.'

He drove back to the office, determined to write a note in his log, but what to write? As he pondered, another thought hit him—she's gone off with my box of tissues. In the end he settled for writing "Something scared the boys" and left it at that. He also wrote a shopping list with 'tissues' at the top.

CHAPTER 12

The Vicar's wife

The vicar's wife, Mrs Prentice, stopped Sam in the street.

'Can I talk to you for a minute?'

She was a woman who was difficult to refuse. Sam had always thought that the vicar had been henpecked, though perhaps he was merely a mild-mannered man.

'Can we go to the station? I'm expecting a call.'

As they walked along the road she said, 'Thanks for looking after Dwayne's mother. Obviously it was difficult for me, she was so distressed and some of it was aimed at me in a way. She seems to be much better since she talked to you.'

'I'm glad to hear it,' said Sam. 'I can't guarantee that level of satisfaction for all my customers.'

At the station she settled into a chair.

'I'm not sure where to begin.'

'Why don't I just sit and listen and you work your way around it. I'm assuming this has to do with William's death.'

She nodded. 'Yes, well that day, certainly.' She paused again. 'I've been fretting over it. Do you know the sort of work I used to help William with?'

'I thought you did visits, organised the flowers, all that sort of thing.'

'Yes, true, I did all that, but before we came here.'

Sam shook his head.

'What do you know about haunting?'

'You mean haunted houses, poltergeists?'

'Those are the movie versions. The real thing is

different. William did some of that work; casting out spirits and exorcism.'

She looked up, meeting his eyes for a moment.

'I used to help him; well he said it helped. It's stressful, you don't know what you're dealing with; you don't even know if you're making a difference. In the end we settled for a quieter life.'

She looked at Sam for encouragement.

'Well, the thing is, um, the way I helped was because William said I was sensitive. I could tell there was something there even when William couldn't.'

Where the hell is this going, thought Sam, but tried to keep a neutral face.

Joyce Prentice took a deep breath and said, 'What did Dwayne's mum say to you?'

'If you hold on I can find my notes.'

'Oh. No, never mind, I wanted to see if she said the same to you as she said to me. It's not telling tales. I mean, I'm not doing something wrong if I tell you am I?'

'We couldn't use it in court because it's hearsay but don't let that bother you. Let's call it intelligence gathering.'

'You weren't there when William spoke were you?'

'I had meant to get there earlier but I arrived just before the explosion.'

'So you didn't hear William's speech?'

'No. Someone said it was strange because he got muddled about which notes he was reading from.'

'Who said that?'

'I forget who.'

'It is sort of true, he did stray off his script but it wasn't the wrong notes, it was something that popped into his head. He said, "Fear is aimless, but evil has direction, so we know which way to face when we fight it. Fear is harder to resist." That's what he said.'

She stopped again and looked straight at Sam.

'When he said it, I had the shivers. Something went right through me, something very awful. It wasn't evil, not an evil spirit; it was like something that was very afraid, primeval, primitive, almost animal. I can't really find words for it.'

Sam watched the colour drain out of her face and tiny beads of sweat appear on her forehead.

'Take your time.'

'No, it's alright, it just came back to me suddenly. Can I have a glass of water?'

Sam fetched a glass. She drank slowly, swallowed twice and her colour came back.

'That's about it really. William finished his speech and then Dwayne came running straight at us saying he'd seen a bogeyman. I nearly said, "So have I", but William grabbed him and came up with that wonderful line about his special collar that kept bogeymen away. Sometimes he could be brilliant like that.'

She stopped, caught somewhere between regret and sadness. A fleeting, wistful smile illuminated her face for a fraction of a second.

'I miss that,' she said, with an air of finality, almost as though closing a mental door. She took another breath.

'Anyway, it did the trick, it broke the spell and Dwayne started to calm down.'

She looked at Sam again, a questioning glance, obviously checking to make sure he didn't think she was crazy.

'I thought I'd better tell you,' she went on. 'I don't know what it was but when Dwayne's mum said both of her boys had seen a bogeyman … she did tell you that didn't she?'

Sam nodded.

'I thought I ought to tell you. I don't know what it was, but there was something very terrible there. I think that young man saw it or felt it too. I only saw him from behind. He wasn't running as though he wanted to get to something or even get away from a person, he was running in desperation as though something awful was after him.'

She dabbed her eyes for a moment.

'I suppose the good news is that it's not there now. I've been back a few times. I've walked all around the area and it's gone. If it was still there I'm sure I'd feel it.'

She smiled for a moment and seemed relieved. She looked at Sam, searching his face for a reaction but got none. She shrugged.

'Well,' she said, 'I've told you now. I don't know what you're going to write down, probably that a mad woman came and talked to you. All I can say is that I am, um, I was the vicar's wife; I've encountered these things before, though never as bad as that. If you're going to believe anyone, you should believe me.'

Sam thought for a moment, thinking that it might be best to say nothing at all but found the words coming out of his mouth.

'This may seem like a daft thing to say, but if an animal encountered something like that, what would happen?'

She thought for a moment, turning the idea over in her mind.

'I think it might drop dead on the spot or maybe run for its life.' She looked up sharply. Again, the searching glance examined Sam but this time she read his thoughts.

'Oh, Farmer Alsop … you don't think?'

Sam tried to look neutral but it was too late.

'It had crossed my mind.'

There was a long pause.

'Be careful,' she said, stopping for a moment and fixing Sam with those startling blue eyes.

'I mean if you try to find it,' she said, 'be careful. Be very, very careful.'

'Don't worry,' he said, trying to lighten the tone and shrug off the fearsome intensity of her gaze. 'It's probably a daft idea. I expect there's some other rational explanation; I'm sure I'll be safe enough.'

For a moment her face seemed to fill his vision. He grinned, laughed a little and tried to find his best village bobby look but he was held in her spell until she broke the contact. She slowly drank the last of the water and handed the glass back to Sam.

'Be very, very … be extremely careful,' she whispered.

CHAPTER 13

Back to the line

Before heading back to the gateway, Sam spent an hour in the local library trying to find out if the obelisk in the hedge had any historical significance, or at least whether anyone had written about it. There was some information about the remains of a Roman camp but a brief study of the map suggested it was on the other side of the next field. Sam made a note but found little else.

It was another day before he had a few spare hours and the chance to explore some more of the line. When he got there he found the farmer ploughing the cornfield, so leaned on the gate for a few minutes until he was noticed. When the tractor came down his side of the field the farmer stopped and strolled over.

'Anything I can help you with?'

'Nothing official, curiosity really. Has this bloody great stone always been here?'

The farmer ran his hand over the stone.

'Big un ain't it? Been here as long as I remember and I was born here. My dad always thought it was one of them megaliths, like Stonehenge. Sometimes wondered if there were more of them but we've never ploughed any up. Might have made a bob or two out of tourists if we'd had half a dozen.'

'Has it always been right here?'

'Never been moved in my lifetime or my dad's. Be a bit bloody hard to shift I reckon but I know what you're coming to, ley lines and the like. We had some of those chaps round here a few years back. Never understood them myself. They said it was lined up on the barrow, summat to do with sunrise or sunset, or it might have been the moon, I forget now.'

'You mean this stone and the barrow lines up with the sun?'

'Or the moon, I forget which. Got to be the right time of year. There was another one over the other side of the hill, long way off apparently; you wouldn't see it through the trees now. I forget where it was but they got very excited. No one ever came back. You know these city types, get them out in the fresh air and they gets all sorts of ideas. That all you wanted, Sam?'

'On that line it looks to me like there was a path or a track or something. The soil's a different colour isn't it?'

'Oh ah, never grows as well. Some years are worse than others, like this year the corn ears were rubbish through there. Grew right enough for a while and then the cobs shrivel up. Ran out of water I reckon, must drain differently. It's not a public right of way or anything but it must have been a track once. Same line as the Roman road except that turns after the camp and takes a different line past the hill.'

'Too steep straight up.'

'Twud be all right on your bike but I can't get a tractor up it. OK for sheep, but that's about it. I'd better get on. You've got sharp eyes seeing that, Sam Diglis. Just as well I s'pose, what with you being a copper, you've got to notice things.'

Sam grinned. If everyone thought that it would probably reduce crime. He watched the tractor set off again, thought about visiting the Roman remains for a moment but headed to the library instead.

An hour later he was back home with Alfred Watkins's little book on 'Old Straight Tracks', but it was evening before he had a chance to read any of it.

The book was small but in many ways hard going because it constantly referred to maps and compass bearings. It also tended to assume that you had an endless supply of one-inch Ordinance Survey maps ready to hand. Sam had local ones but, unfortunately, Watkins did not seem to have visited this area. No matter, the gist of it was what mattered. Watkins's theory was that the landscape was full of old tracks that tended to be straight and they were often marked by things like standing stones, burial mounds and natural landscape features. The book was written before the Second World War, so Watkins had no access to computers. In fact, he seemed to have done most of the work himself and the writing gave no hint of academic discipline. There was plenty of recorded observation but not much in the way of theory behind it. If you took what Watkins had learned from one line, or even ten, it didn't really give you any clues about why that line had been chosen or where the next one would be.

The next day Sam got up early and spent an hour on the internet, trying to get beyond Watkins's simple observations. One way or another he kept coming back to two questions. If I find a few landmarks that are lined up, how do I know if it is a ley line or a coincidence; and if it is a ley line, so what? What does it mean?

Those questions kept the line in Sam's mind for the next few days and every morning he'd look at it on the map. He was halfway through a sausage one breakfast time when he remembered his conversation at the gate with the farmer.

"There was another one over the other side of the hill, long way off apparently." He traced the line down the hill on his one-inch map and kept going across the page. Eight inches from the hill he hit the straight track to the farm that was suspected of housing smugglers. He remembered that he'd half promised Ashton and Small that he would visit. It seemed like a good excuse and he had an hour free. He parked on the road where the farm track started. Not wanting to arouse suspicion he unpacked a sandwich and sat on the bike eating. It didn't need acute observation skills to see a seven-foot vertical stone standing in the corner of the hedge at the beginning of the track. He kicked himself for not thinking of it before. Attached to the stone was a sign, "Old Stone Farm".

He turned the bike around, parked next to the stone and stood up on the footrests to look back at the ridge. He took a compass bearing and, sure enough, it hit the ridge right exactly at the notch where he knew the barrow nestled on the other side of the hill.

When he got back to the station he phoned Ashton and Small.

'Have you ever heard of ley lines?'

'Some sort of mystic stuff isn't it? Are you going all New Age on us?'

'No, but I had an idea about your surveillance.'

'Gonna do it by dowsing or something?'

'No, better than that. Old Stone Farm is bang on a ley line and the stone in question is an ancient marker and sits at the top of the lane to the farm. It's one of those things archaeologists get worked up about. I figured you could use it as cover. Turn up there with surveying kit, look a bit mystical and you could probably plant a camera or something.'

'You're kidding?'

'No seriously. I was talking to a farmer on the other side of the hill. He's got a similar stone, only he's got a gate hung on his. He had some nerds from the city turn up a few years ago, measuring things. I guess it's too much to expect you two to look intelligent but maybe you could borrow someone from another patch? Preferably from a manor where your villains have never been seen.'

He could feel them bristling at the other end of the

phone.

'We'll think about it, Sam. While you were exploring the local monuments did you happen to see anything suspicious?'

'No. The weather's been too dry, no sign of unusual tracks and no white vans. Give it some thought, guys. You could stick a camera in the hedge, probably run for a week. A lot easier than trying to stake it out yourselves. It's a poor area for that sort of thing.'

'Meaning what?'

'You can't buy a pizza for miles for starters. The nearest high ground is several miles away. You might manage a telescope from there but you're unlikely to get anything of evidence quality at that range. Anywhere nearer and you'd look dead obvious.'

Sam left it at that. It was up to them now. There was a curious satisfaction about finding Old Stone Farm on the same line as the other events. In a way, it seemed to justify his curiosity in following the line.

CHAPTER 14

Post-mortem

To say that Maria burst in would be an exaggeration, she's not like that, thought Sam, but it felt as though she were ready to explode.

'Did you know?' she said.

'Know what?'

'About the post-mortem.'

A quick glance at Maria's face brought him up short, the strain was obvious and he suspected she'd been crying. More than that he thought, she's not been getting enough sleep.

'I told you all about it. I went through it with the pathologist.'

'No, not that one, the second one.'

'I didn't know there was a second one.'

She deflated a little and pulled a letter out of her handbag.

'There isn't yet but there's going to be. We can't bury John until they've done it.'

Sam took the letter from her hand and read it. When he put it down she said, 'I can't stop them can I.' It wasn't a question; there was a note of resignation creeping into her voice.

'I suppose they're asking for a second PM because it could have serious consequences for Mr Sanders. He could lose his licence or even go to prison.'

'But what could they hope to find?'

'I don't know. I don't even know if I'm supposed to talk to you about it.'

'I didn't come for a lecture. You have experience of

these things and I haven't, that's why I'm here. I can't go wasting money on hiring a lawyer to argue with them.'

'OK, this time I'll make the tea.' This is going to take time, he thought. He shut the front door and put up the sign giving the public the number to ring when the station was closed, led Maria into a back room and then he made tea.

'Let's start with the basics. Why does it matter? Do you have arrangements made?'

'No, but we might have. I don't like John being there in that fridge but I can put up with it while it's necessary. It's not because I'm squeamish about post-mortems either, it's my daughter, Anna. It's driving her crazy. She hasn't taken any of this very well and now we get a letter saying they won't release the body until they've cut him up again. She cries all the time, keeps on about cold slabs and "first they smash him up and now they want to cut him up". Is there nothing we can do?'

'It would need a lawyer to know all the loopholes, I can't be sure. If there wasn't the possibility of prosecution then I'm sure you could object but this is potentially a criminal case and the defence has rights.'

'But what could they hope to find?'

'You sure you want to hear this?'

She gave him a sharp look.

'OK, OK. You're here, enough said. John could have been drunk, he could have been on drugs.'

He saw her face change.

'Oh for heavens sake, he was only taking the dog for a walk and anyway, alcohol only needs a blood test and they probably already did that.'

'More to the point, I suppose, is the severity of the injuries. It gives some sort of guide how fast the car was going when it hit John, so if the coroner's pathologist had overestimated the severity, then it might lead a jury to conclude that the car was speeding and that would obviously make a conviction more likely.'

'So there's nothing I can say to Anna?'

'Not really. It's a horrible thing and they don't exactly teach this in school. I doubt if anyone knows the procedure on these things until they run up against it. I know you hear politicians going on about victims' rights, but much of the law is about being fair to suspects so that there isn't a miscarriage of justice. I'm sorry, I doubt if Anna is likely to feel much sympathy for due process and legal precedent. It's one of those things that has to be got through.'

There was a long pause.

'It's not good, Sam. It twists me around. I felt sorry for Mr Sanders before but now I think he's a cruel bastard.'

'He may not even know.'

'What?'

'It may be something that his lawyers dreamed up. They do that sort of thing.'

There was another long pause.

'Are you just saying that?'

'No, I'm serious. I've seen it happen.'

'This gets worse,' she said. 'OK even if I believe you, but it doesn't make it any easier. What am I going to do about Anna?'

'Are you sure I'm the right person for this? Shouldn't you be talking to a social worker?'

'Oh, I know, yes of course, but if Anna gets wind of a social worker somewhere in the wings she'll go bananas. At least with you it's obvious why I ought to talk to you. My husband's killed in a car crash, so obviously I'm talking to the police.'

She looked at him with an almost sly smile.

'Maybe you should talk to a social worker and then she can tell you how to deal with the mad woman at the end of the lane.'

'You're not mad.'

From the way she looked at him, he half expected her to say, "not yet".

'What exactly is the problem with Anna?'

'I hardly know where to begin. She is completely distraught about her dad. I probably don't help, it's not as though I'm totally fine myself.' She paused for a second and in that instant Sam caught a glimpse of what might be going on behind that brave face. Before he could think what to say, she was back in her stride.

'Right at the bottom of it, Anna feels as though there are things she wished she'd been able to tell him. It's probably her age. Do you have any idea what teenage girls are like?'

'I have some relatives.'

'It's a time when everything changes very fast. She can tell me about it but she wants to tell her dad. She doesn't want to upset me. It's complicated.'

Maria paused for a moment. He could almost hear the thoughts spinning around in her head. She's been crying at night and Anna knows, so I'm the middle man.

'Do you believe in psychics?' she said.

'Sorry, bit of a blank canvas there. I've not had to think about it one way or another. I've come across a few con artists but that doesn't mean it's all fake.'

'Anna is trying to contact her dad. She spends every spare minute reading that stuff and I know she's talked to some people who are into it. She's all over the internet with it. I don't know where it will end and I'm worried sick.'

She stopped again. At least this time she had her own tissues, Sam thought, having glanced at the box and remembered, it was Dwayne's mother who took the last lot; there were too many grieving women in his life.

'I feel awful myself,' she said. 'I'm still crying buckets but I'm so worried about her. She's so vulnerable.'

Sam played for time and poured more tea. Maybe he did need that social worker after all. When he sat down again he only had one idea but it would have to do for now.

'I'm out of my depth on this', said Sam. 'I need time to think about it and we probably need to talk some more if you can cope with that. One thing I can suggest is that if you find names of particular people or organisations that you think she's getting too close to or that you're worried about, then I can check them out and make sure they haven't got form. I've no idea if there are genuine people out there who can help but we could at least keep her away from crooks.'

He could see the relief on Maria's face.

'See, I knew you were the one to talk to. I'll be back, I'm sure. I'll try not to bother you too often. Thanks so much.'

CHAPTER 15

Surveillance

Ashton and Small spent some time deliberating, mostly because they had no idea what Sam had been talking about and wondered if it was some sort of wind up. Neither of them felt sufficiently confident in themselves that they could afford to be the butt of a practical joke. Eventually they did find someone at the university who could be persuaded to go and look at the stone. He was able to promise various pieces of scientific apparatus and a few days later visited the stone at the entrance to the farm lane.

The research student scraped some loose pieces from the base and shoved a probe underneath it to get a soil sample without disturbing anything else. He had put these samples in bags and was finding an accurate geo-position when Farmer Garside appeared. After a few polite exchanges during which the student attempted to explain what he was doing, he was told to push off.

The student, warming to the task, waved various letters around, attempting to demonstrate his credentials as a scientist and elicit sympathy by saying how important all this was to his research project.

All he achieved was that the frequency of swear words, and various other agricultural phrases, increased markedly.

'But I'm not trespassing, this is part of the highway.'

'That don't stop me telling you to shift your arse.'

'You've got no right to make me leave.'

'You tell your precious professor it's health and

safety. Your health and your safety. If you aren't out of here in five minutes, a bloody great tractor is going to run over your foot and crunch up your clever bloody equipment into tiny little pieces.'

The student duly reported back to Ashton and Small and gratefully accepted his fee.

'Was it worth doing? Did you get what you wanted?' said the student.

'Can't say too much, hush, hush, you see,' said Ashton. 'Make sure you don't tell a soul. The one thing we do know now is that yon farmer is very touchy and doesn't want anyone snooping around near his farm.'

'Has to mean something,' said Small. 'That's a result.'

They quizzed the student for a while about ley lines, not wanting to be outflanked by Sam again.

'It depends who you want to believe.'

'Don't come all that academic, on the one hand, on the other hand stuff. Give us the five-minute version.'

'A chap called Alfred Watkins, back in the nineteen twenties, developed a theory about ancient tracks. They tended to be straight and were often marked by standing stones, like the one you sent me to, or burial mounds and sometimes bits of landscape such as tops of hill, notches on the side of hills. The sort of thing you can see from a long way off. He thought they must have been trade routes or maybe something ceremonial. He called them ley lines.'

'What's so clever about that?'

'After Watkins it got more complicated; people started attaching mystical significance to the lines. Some of them follow the line of sunrise or moonrise, like Stonehenge. You've heard of that?'

'Who hasn't. Druids and all that stuff.'

'Exactly. So, some people have theories about earth energy flowing along the line, though no one has said exactly what this energy is. There has been some fashion for dowsing, you know, like for water, but for some of this energy. Some people want to link it all to astronomy because of the sunrise connection, and from there you are only one step away from flying saucers and who knows what else.'

'You sound a bit sceptical.'

'Dead right. Most of my thesis is about proving that it's all a load of rubbish.'

'So Sam's off his head about it?'

A hint of doubt was visible in the student's face.

'What did your colleague actually say?'

There was a pause while the two detectives looked at each other.

Small looked at Ashton. 'You talked to him.'

'He said the stone was on a ley line that went over the hill to another stone.'

'That is true. It follows the line of the Roman road further up. Ley lines often do, though I think the ancient tracks were there before the Romans.'

'He said people would be interested in it. Like who?'

The student grinned.

'Not everyone of course, but ley lines are studied obsessionally by some people. From what you said before it sounds to me as though your mate didn't say that he believed in any theories about it. He was just giving you a way to put someone on the ground.'

'Well, yeah.'

'Only one problem then,' said the student, trying to suppress a grin.

'What's that?' said Small.

'It's blown now. You can't exactly send someone else back with the same cover as me; Garside told me to 'F' off.'

'Yeah, true, but at least we know there's a good chance he's up to no good.'

The student grinned at them again.

'Your man Sam sounds like he's smart.'

'Yeah, too smart. I bet he does believe in all that mumbo jumbo, we can rib him about it anyway.'

'Is that fair?'

'Sorry, not your problem. Time you were going. Thanks for the help, it's given us the lead we need. We'll take it from here.'

Once the student had left the building, the two detectives settled down to work out their next move. It didn't take long to decide that Sam was right about the lack of cover. There wasn't a building within a mile and no obvious place where someone could hide to stake out the farm buildings.

'We'll have to do a drive by.'

'Just to case the joint you mean? We can't hang about there if Garside is paranoid.'

'We could break down and wait for the AA.'

'Yeah and take the chance on him being a mechanical genius and pitching up with a spanner and sending us on our way? There's half a chance his chums have got the numbers of all the cop cars on the patch.'

An hour later they were back in the office and staring at a new set of pictures on the computer screen.

Eventually it was Small who said, 'Hey, I've got an idea. What about the telephone poles? We could get a maintenance crew along, you know, one of those tower wagons and work our way along each of the poles.'

'What and look like real British workers and take all day about it? We can't keep that up for weeks.'

'No, we'll stick a camera on top of one of the poles. We'd get a brilliant view from up there, better than Sam's idea of one in the hedge. Let's get the tech people on it. I bet they'd have a way of running a video from the telephone power, or maybe a bloody big battery.'

'Or a solar panel maybe.'

'I bet they could get something permanent up there. Think about it, if we take our time and work our way along all the poles, we could get an extra wire in, run power, get a continuous feed. It wouldn't need any radio or anything they might spot, or jam or anything. Even if it takes a day to two, we'd get a brilliant result.'

'Specially now we've got a probable from what our young friend did for us.'

Would they arouse suspicion that the farm's phone was going to be tapped? Fortunately, this was dismissed when they discovered that Garside had not paid his phone bill. To add to the cover story, a few days beforehand they sent a letter to "The Occupier" at Old Stone Farm saying that routine servicing was being carried out on the phone lines and they would do their best to minimise disruption to the telephone service.

Ashton regretted not being able to bug the farm to hear Garside's reaction to the letter, but you can't have fun everyday.

Sticking to the cover story, they started work a couple of miles away and worked towards the farm. As expected, they found a source of power and within a week had a camera feeding back pictures with a good view of the lane up to the farm. Any vehicle going in or out was bound to be caught on tape now. After that, it was a waiting game. Ashton and Small decided that action was most likely after dark. The camera had an infra red setting so they sat up most of the night watching nothing happen.

Four nights and gallons of coffee later, a container truck rolled down the lane and disappeared into the big barn.

Small stayed glued to the screen while Ashton interrogated crime reports. Twenty minutes later they had identified the truck, a container load of cigarettes hijacked on the motorway.

They put the rest of the squad on standby and in an hour had plain cars hidden a mile away while they waited for the vans to arrive.

'We could pile in and grab them now.'

'That way we'll only get the little people. Right now, there are probably a couple of nobodies in there splitting the load. They'll have it in segments that will go nicely into white vans.'

'There's no guarantee any of the big boys will go anywhere near the place; they'll be miles away pulling strings.'

'Ashton, wake up, that's not the point. Wait until the vans arrive and we mop up the distribution system. We follow each of the vans in and out and nail them there and then, or maybe follow them to somewhere peaceful where they're not expecting it. We can clean up the farm; they can't move the big truck without us seeing it. We make sure we get the vans, excise will get the big boys.'

'You don't know how many vans there might be. What if we can't follow them all?'

'We wade in and nab them.'

'You're making this up as you go along,' said Ashton, trying to keep his end up.

'There's nothing wrong with that. Flexible, that's what I am. We know the truck is stolen so we can do them for something. We're sure of a collar, but we need to make it as big as we can. The more of them we nick, the better chance one of them will talk and lead us to some more. Look on the bright side, we're in business.'

Half an hour later, Small was watching the screen as the first few vans arrived. They were not all white.

'How many vans could you load from one container?'

'Six or eight I reckon, maybe more.'

'We'd better hang on a bit longer then.'

In another twenty minutes, there were six vans and they got a lucky break when the doors to the barn stayed open and they could glimpse the activity inside. Finally, they had clear evidence of materials being unloaded from the container and into the vans.

Small phoned the excise men and they all agreed that now was the time to move in. Catching six van drivers and Garside red handed ought to give them enough leverage in any interrogation and they were bound to pick up more of the connections upstream, even if the big boys were not on site. As he was speaking something happened. In the picture, they could see signs of movement. One of the vans suddenly backed out at speed and figures could be seen running.

Ashton got on the radio.

'Something's spooked them. Lots of activity, move in, block the lane, be ready for anything. We've got all the film we need, grab the lot of them.'

Ashton watched, fascinated, as one van crashed into another, spinning it around before setting off at speed down the lane. Would the interceptors get there in time? The van that had spun, reversed, turned and set off after the first. In the barn there was still plenty of action but even with the light spilling out it was hard to see what was happening.

'It looks as though they're fighting. That guy at the side of the building, has he got a gun?'

Small stared at the screen, craning forwards and shielding his eyes, trying to get a better view.

'You're right, I'm sure that was a flash. He's shooting at something inside the barn.'

Two figures came out of the side door, both running towards the lane as another van backed out at speed. The shooter ran towards the van as it stopped reversing and started to pull forwards. He leapt in.

Ashton got on the radio.

'Third van coming up the lane, passenger looks like he has a gun.'

As he spoke the light changed and seconds later, a gush of flame came out of the side door. More figures could be seen running and then there were flames coming out of the big doors.

'The place is on fire, there's still three vans and the truck inside.'

As Ashton called on the radio, Small talked to the fire brigade.

'Big barn on a farm, full of smuggled tobacco and who knows what else. It's already burning.'

'Do we get down there or keep watching from here?' said Ashton.

'We should get down there. We should have got a video feed to a car.'

'Yeah well I'm glad we didn't,' said Ashton. 'The boss would have had us sleeping in the car for the last week. Hang on a sec' and see what happens. We can't get there before those vans are down the lane.'

Ashton panned the camera around, blocking Small's view as he concentrated on getting the angle right. He could see the interceptors make it to the start of the lane—two police cars side by side completely blocking the road. One of the occupants leapt out, ran forwards a few yards and threw something across the road.

'What are they doing now?' said Small, trying to shove him out of the way to get a look at the screen.

'He's put a stinger down, if that front van doesn't stop he'll have no tyres.'

'Yeah and that will make it hard to stop.' Small finally got a view of the picture. 'He should have put it further down the road.'

'I bet he knows what he's doing—well maybe not,' said Ashton as the van ran over the stinger, swerved uncontrollably and crashed into the police cars. The second van was only yards behind and joined the wreckage seconds later.

The third van had time to see the others crash. As they watched they could see it speed up and then a few yards before the wreckage it swung sideways and headed for the hedge, flattening everything in its path until it made it into the field. The ground had been ploughed, so apart from a small strip at the edge there was little chance of making it across to a gateway. The van picked up speed alongside the hedge and then crashed into the hedgerow at the corner of the field aiming to break through to the road. At that point local knowledge or a belief in ley lines would have helped as they hit the standing stone almost full on. Seven feet of solid rock, put there thousands of years ago to do a job that no one now remembered. That made no difference. The rock planned to go on doing what it did best, standing very still.

'If the bloke with the shooter is in the passenger seat, I don't reckon he'll be doing much shooting.'

'There is one little problem, Ashton me old mate.'

'What?'

'There's a dirty great fire engine gonna want to get down that lane in about three minutes. He might have a bit of a problem.'

Small's estimate was correct. The police had arrested the various occupants of the first two vans, who were now cuffed and in the back of the two squad cars, but the first van had managed to hit both cars and crush a wing into the front wheels of both of them.

Ashton and Small decided they had better get down to the farm and by the time they arrived the fire engine had pulled the last of the wrecks out of the way. Another police van and an ambulance arrived. The driver was dragged out of the van that was wrapped around the big stone and stretchered over to the ambulance. His passenger was dead. The paramedics called for more help and tried to deal with the casualties. Two policemen stayed to supervise the arrested crooks while the rest of the squad prepared to follow the fire engine down the road towards the blazing barn.

They arrived to find one man desperately aiming a hose at the burning barn and another trying to soak the nearest building in the hope of stopping the fire spreading. Garside, the farmer, was driving a tractor with a front bucket, trying to push or pull pieces of equipment out of range of the flames. They were all a little astonished to be arrested on the spot by armed police but at least the fire brigade were on hand.

Ashton took one look and said to Small, 'There's something wrong here. There's not enough of them. Did any leg it over the fields?'

'Didn't see any.'

'You do the maths. There's two cars parked over there, one of them might be Garside's, and there were six vans and the truck. We haven't got enough drivers. There ought to be eight of them beside Garside and I can only account for seven including Garside. Who have we got in the squad car?'

'"That one nearest us?'

'Yeah.'

'Garside and a couple of blokes out of the crashed vans.'

'Right,' said Ashton, marching over to the squad car and opening the door.

'How many people are still in the barn?'

'Three or four.'

The three men looked at each other. Ashton didn't give them a chance to confer.

'It's your farm, Garside, what happened?

'It was all so fast, I don't really know. I was outside and then the yelling and shooting started. The next thing I know there's flames and people running for it.'

'Oh come on,' said Ashton, 'you can't have all been outside. You,' he said, pointing to the one sitting in the middle, 'what were you doing? We know you were taking stolen fags out of a hijacked lorry, so you can skip the innocent, who me stuff; what were you doing?'

'My van was parked at the side of the truck. The truck driver and his mate had already unloaded some; they had one of those little forklifts like they hook on the back of trucks. I was loading my van. I was the first one here, worst luck, so I was bound to be out last.'

'Tough. What happened?'

'I don't want to sound stupid but I don't really know. The bloke who drives that black van, or his mate, not sure which, started shouting. Said he'd seen something in the truck. Didn't make sense, it was a sealed container. There couldn't be anyone in there but the way he was behaving it was like there was a wild animal or something. Next thing I know his mate is raving too, shouting, "Get back, get back." I couldn't see too well because there was another van in the way. Next thing I knew he was shooting. I didn't even know they had guns. I don't know what he was shooting at. He obviously got the wind up about something.'

He sat shaking his head for a few seconds.

'I don't know what he hit. I mean, shooting blind in a barn, fucking stupid.'

He looked at Garside.

'He's the farmer. I don't know what was in the barn, you ask him, but something exploded and after that it was mayhem. We were all trying to run for it, the idiot with the gun was shooting, two of the vans decided to make a run for it and they crashed into each other. I was lucky to get out.'

'Your turn, Garside, what did he hit? You keeping home made bombs in there?'

'Could have been the welding kit, maybe. There was some diesel too, that burns, but not usually like that. If a lucky shot blew the valve off the welder, anything could happen. I'd just like to know what he was shooting at.'

'That's the one thing we might not find out.'

'Why don't you ask him? You must have caught

them.'

'We did, but your trigger happy friend won't be talking because they smashed his side of the van into that big stone the farm's named after.'

There was a long silence. Eventually Ashton said, 'You boys sit and think about it.' He closed the door, walked back to the fire engine and found the man in charge.

'I think there might be some blokes still inside.'

'Shit. Any idea how many?'

'Three or four they said.'

'You mean they don't know for sure?'

'They're bloody clueless but I reckon there's still some inside.'

'There's no way my boys are going in to that. If there was anyone in there they don't stand a chance unless there's a cellar or something, but even then, I doubt it. We're making progress but it'll be too hot to touch for hours yet.'

'Right. Tell your lads it's a crime scene so put the fire out and leave the rest to us.'

CHAPTER 16

Old Stone Farm

By the time Sam got the call from Ashton and Small he had already picked up some news on the grapevine that there had been a major incident at Old Stone Farm.

'It was bloody mayhem,' said Ashton. 'Hard to say what happened. We've had the place guarded overnight, we're still tied up with the people we arrested and forensics are down at the farm. If the barn's cooled down enough we may find out how many bodies are still inside.'

'Mind if I have a look?'

'Feel free. Your ley lines are a bit buggered up. One of the vans smashed into the big stone; killed the passenger.'

'That's not strictly part of the line, it's a marker, that's all. Sounds bad all the same.'

Rick Small came on the line. 'Take a shufti if you want, Sam. We've nailed the smugglers but the coroner's going to have fun putting a verdict on whoever's inside, unless any of them turn out to be shot. The shooter was the fatality so we have no idea what he was firing at. Do your ley lines make guns go off?'

'I'm never going to live this down am I?'

'Not if we can help it.'

Sam laughed and put the phone down, picked up his bag and set off for the farm.

The building was burned out and still steaming and smoking in places. The roof had collapsed but there was no mistaking the container lorry and two vans among the wreckage. The third van was outside, but burned out with its rear doors buckled.

Sam walked around the smoking remains and then spent the next hour working with the forensic team, carefully picking through the wreckage, photographing and recording each item as they identified it. Farmer Garside's tractor still worked, so using the front loader they gradually prised loose the remains of the roof and piled the corrugated iron sheets at a safe distance. The container on the back of the truck was buckled but still intact.

They found the first body in the container, amidst the partially burned remains of some of the cigarette load. Sealed in the container, the cargo had burned all the oxygen and rendered most of what was left into charcoal. They marked the position of the body and then carefully extracted it into a body bag to take to the mortuary.

Another body was by the door at the side of the building. It looked as though he had been crawling towards the door. They turned the body over as they tried to roll it into the bag and because the man had fallen face down his chest was not burned so the bullet hole was obvious.

They searched for more bodies, but the space was cramped between the vehicles so they hauled the two vans out of the wreckage, which at least gave them a chance to examine the container lorry from all sides. The last body was underneath the truck. Fortunately that one was not extensively burned. Probably suffocated in the heat with all the oxygen consumed by the fire, thought Sam. They dragged the body out, got it into a bag and sent all three off to the morgue for the coroner to investigate.

'Can we piece this jigsaw together?' said Sam.

'Man in the van outside starts shooting. One guy hides in container, can't say if he's been shot. Chap on the left gets shot in the chest, tries to make it to the door, collapses on the way, chances are that the coroner will find his chest wound is fatal. Body three hides under the lorry, safe from the shooter, but not from the fire.'

'What caused the fire?'

'The welding gear over there is damaged; looks like a bullet hit the regulator. Was that before body two got it or after? My money is on after. First shot gets the bloke—he tries to make for the door, shooter aims at him again, misses by a fraction and hits welder, boom, way to the door is blocked, bloke collapses. What we don't know is how many shots he fired and why he started shooting. How am I doing?'

'Not bad so far,' said Sam. 'There's two bullet holes at the end of the container, so it seems like he saw something in there and started shooting at it.'

'Could have been the man in the container.'

'Could have, but why did the shooter shoot and why did he run? He'd dropped one of them, maybe two and the place was on fire. Anyone else coming out was a sitting duck but he didn't wait for them, instead, him and his mate get in the van and run.'

'They're thugs, Sam, who knows how their minds work.'

'It doesn't wash. What about the first two vans? If the shooter was after everyone else, making a play to grab all of the loot or whatever, why did he let them go?'

'Maybe they were just quick off the mark.'

'No they weren't. One van crashed into the other while they were turning, the shooter had plenty of time to nail them. He let them go.'

There was silence as Sam walked to a spot facing the barn.

'You've looked at the tape, he was standing about here, right?'

'A few yards to the right I think.'

Sam moved over and then bent down and picked up a cartridge case. He looked around and picked up two more and then another. He scoured the ground around him.

'Four shells, two hit the truck, which is hard to miss at this range, one dead body and a welding machine. That could almost be random, I wonder what he was aiming at? Oh hang on here's another.' He placed it in the evidence bag along with the first four.

'He moved forwards a pace, no, back a pace while he was shooting. I think on the tape it was backwards and the van came across in front of him and he jumped in.'

Sam stepped back a yard or two.

'We need to look at the tape again but I think it goes like this. People run out of the barn, four of them together. Three of them dash to the vans and they are in a serious panic because two crash into each other. The third backs away and then turns across in front of the barn, picks up the shooter and burns rubber.'

The forensic man took the bag from Sam.

'These aren't all the same gun, the last one is a different calibre.'

'I think the shooter was giving covering fire,' said Sam. 'He was shooting at something in the barn to keep it at bay while the others got away. I think the other gun was with the driver of the third van. I think he fired once while he stopped to let the first shooter get into the van.'

'They didn't recover any guns from any of the vans.'

'I reckon they chucked them as they went down the lane. Probably when they saw the blue lights. Nice game for someone with a metal detector. A stroll down the lane might be productive; have to do both sides and find a way to get into the hedge. Got to be worth a go.'

'OK Sam, nice story. Only question is, what were

they running from?'

Something very evil and scary, thought Sam.

'Who knows. They were probably feeling a bit hyper - truck load of fags, complicated operation, six vans all in a hurry, maybe the fumes from all the tobacco got to them, maybe they were pissed, or snorting coke? We might get something out of the first two van drivers. Van three is a dead loss, the main shooter is dead and the driver is still out to the world and probably won't remember a thing even if we show him the footage from our surveillance camera. He's had a big enough bang on the head to forget Christmas but the other two don't have the same excuse.'

'It's not Christmas yet, Sam.'

'It will be before that guy wakes up.'

CHAPTER 17

Maria again

When Sam got home he almost ran to his wall map. The idea had been bugging him since the conversation at the farm but it was almost four in the afternoon before he had a chance to look at the map. He carefully measured the distance from the jumble sale to Alsop's farm, then to the car crash site and finally to Old Stone Farm. He did some arithmetic before sitting down and repeating the calculation carefully, making sure to write down every step of the calculation.

'Bang on time,' he said out loud, 'I should have thought of it before.'

'Should have thought of what before?' said a voice behind him. He turned, saw no one but realised he had left the front door open. He found Maria Roberts standing there.

'Sorry to intrude,' she said. 'I saw you come in and followed you because I wanted a word. I'm obviously interrupting something. I can come back later.'

'No, really it's OK, I was working something out, I think I'm done now.'

'Can I come in? Is it OK to talk here or do I need to go to the station?'

'There's only me that'll know. As long as you behave yourself, I guess there's no problem. You'll be needing a cup of tea I expect, so come on in.'

As Sam made tea Maria said, 'Am I allowed to look at the map?'

'There's not much on there that you couldn't get from the newspapers. It's really to remind me not to forget anything.'

Maria was still examining the map when Sam returned with two mugs of tea.

'Now, what can I do for you?'

'I was talking to my sister and something she said worried me. I wondered what she had been telling you.'

'Your sister?'

'Joyce Prentice, William Prentice's wife. The vicar's wife.'

'I hadn't realised. Now you mention it, I guess there is a family likeness.'

'She said you were interested in exorcisms, which probably meant she'd been going on at you about it. It's one of those subjects with her; once she gets going on it, she seems to lose her sense of perspective.'

'She did mention it.'

Maria smiled.

'Very diplomatic. I was worried that she was putting the jumble sale business down to ghosts or something. She's told me several times that she had one of her feelings. I know she has to get it out of her system and I feel terrible about what happened, but I don't want her getting in the way of proper detective work.'

'She's only talked to me; the people who are doing the wider enquiries haven't spoken to her. Actually, between you and me they're not the sorts to go for a story like that. They can be a bit one-dimensional. Don't worry about it. How's your daughter getting on?'

'Not very well. Now she feels guilty about the dog, feels if she hadn't gone on about getting a dog we'd never have got one. Worse still, she thinks it should have been her walking the dog and then she'd have been killed instead of John. She's still obsessed with finding some way to talk to him.'

She stopped for a moment and Sam was ready to reach for the tissues.

'It's all awful,' she said. 'Joyce is no help with Anna,

encourages her even. William kept Joyce's feet on the ground and stopped her getting too "spiritual". He was very good like that. Funny thing is I think she only fell for him because he'd done exorcisms.' She paused again for a moment. 'I'm no help because I feel guilty about Joyce. They'd never have moved here if it wasn't for me.'

'Do you get the same feelings Joyce has? On the night of the accident you said you had a premonition.'

'I suppose, though not as much. I tend to ignore it. I've always been more practical, I don't let it run my life. Well, that's not fair really. Joyce is sensible most of the time but she can let it run away with her.'

'OK, I shouldn't have asked,' he said, 'but I can't help tying off loose ends. I know it's not always helpful to be logical but I'll try. John being exactly where he was has to have been pure chance. If the dog had stopped to pee, or if it hadn't, if anything had made John get there half a minute either way, then the car would have missed him. If he'd bent down to tie his shoelace the car would have gone over his head; it missed the dog and the lead was only a yard long, it had to have gone right over the dog.'

Maria nodded.

'I know, I know, I've told myself that a hundred times. I suppose I'll listen eventually.'

'There are plenty of ways that "if only" comes up with William's death too—if the old lady had not had her little heater, for instance, then the fire would never have started. I won't go on. Somehow both of you need to get "if only" out of your heads.'

Sam watched her absorb what he was saying and then gradually her gaze shifted and she was looking past him at the map.

'That line on the map, what is it?'

'Something one of the farmers was telling me about, it's an old ley line.'

'And John and William's deaths are both on it? That's a hell of coincidence isn't it? Two deadly accidents connected by something thousands of years old. Joyce didn't see that map did she?'

'No, she hasn't been here.'

'Thank heavens for small mercies, that would have set her off completely.'

'Why?'

'Oh come on, two deaths that close together and on a ley line, it's right up her street.'

'What if there were four incidents?'

'What?' She almost jumped out of her seat. In two steps, she was standing next to the map, trying to read Sam's notes.

'My God, Farmer Alsop is on the same line?'

'Plus last night's fracas.'

'Last night?'

'A shooting, a fire and a car crash at Old Stone Farm. Here on the map. Right on the line.'

'That sounds dreadful.'

'You'll probably read about it in the papers, one of them is in the ITU at your hospital and four are in the morgue. They hijacked a lorry full of cigarettes and were unloading the cargo into smaller vans in a big barn on the farm when something went wrong.'

Maria managed to look shocked and confused at the same time.

'That's terrible … but it doesn't sound mysterious. Was there a rival gang?'

Sam took a long swig of tea.

'It doesn't look like it. Obviously we don't have anything out of the witnesses yet and who knows whether we can rely on what they have to say. What's bothering me is that it looks as though they were scared by something; something that caused them to run for their lives. Two of them shot at it, whatever it was and one of the shots caused the fire. After that it went from bad to worse. The fire trapped three of them and another was killed when a speeding van crashed. A more rational theory might be that they fell out among themselves and that's what caused the shots to be fired. I imagine that's what the inquest will decide. The only problem with that theory is that they started running before the shooting and it was the ones with guns who were running away. Running without any of the loot I might add.'

'How do you know they ran first?' said Maria.

'Promise you won't tell.'

'Yes of course.'

'Really?'

'Yes. Sam you've already been very helpful over John's death, I'm not going to put that at risk.'

'We had a video camera, long range, but good enough to see what was happening.'

He stopped for a moment, drank some more tea and went on.

'Don't tell Joyce about this. I reckon you know enough about what she would think but you're the sceptical one. It would help a lot if I could have a bit of that because I'm looking at four violent episodes and in each one someone reacted like they'd seen a ghost and did something that caused a tragedy. They all happened on this line and if you do the maths, which I've done about five times, the distance apart is almost exactly proportional to the time between them. It's as though something was moving along that line, going quite slowly, about a half mile a day. Somehow it gets into the heads of people or animals who are passing by and blows their mind.'

'Four in a row.'

'Each one right on the timeline.'

Maria's face paled.

'Even if you wanted me to, I wouldn't dare tell Joyce. She'd be off down that line, doing her sensitive thing and trying to feel for it. Who knows what would happen then and we don't have William to cast out the demons.'

'This may sound like a daft question but if William did cast them out, have you any idea where they went?'

To Sam's relief, she smiled, almost laughed.

'I asked him that once. I can't say he gave the clearest of answers. Joyce could give you biblical quotes. The demons are cast into the void, which probably means hell, or they go into someone else or hang around looking for someone else. Does any of that help?'

'I've looked into some of that but it doesn't seem like the same sort of thing. The people who have been affected were scared. It's not as if some demon was making them do bad things, they were very frightened and wanted to get away. If William and Joyce thought they'd been successful, how did they know?'

'I think neither of them could feel it anymore.'

'So they didn't follow the demon to somewhere else or see it go?'

Maria sighed. 'You'd have to ask Joyce but I'd rather you didn't, at least not 'til you're sure what you are looking for.'

'That may take me a while,' said Sam. 'Right now I'm probably the only person who thinks it's even worth looking at.'

'And me,' she said and suddenly smiled. 'Hey, here's a thought. If that timeline means anything, it tells us we are safe now. Whatever it was has gone past, so as long as we don't go down here,' she pointed at the map, 'then we're safe.'

'Yeah, but the people down there may not be.'

She looked at his grim face and knew there was no point in telling him not to go after it.

CHAPTER 18

Cross-country

Something about the headline "Record Breaking Run" caught Sam's eye. Four boys broke the school cross-country record.

A teacher was quoted as saying, "One boy breaking the record is unusual but four going through the old record in one race is truly exceptional. They ran like the devil was at their heels."

That phrase stuck in Sam's mind. Next question, where was the run?

It was easy enough to identify the school, that was in the newspaper report, but he couldn't simply stroll up as the village bobby and ask about the cross-country. What possible reason could he have?

He found the school on the map, several miles away from the line. Back to that question—how wide was the line, if it existed at all?

More searching on the internet found an article about dowsing on ley lines. The author thought they were about seven yards wide, though sometimes stretching to a hundred. That was still a long way away from the school. A cross country run, on the other hand, had to be in the country, so was there any way of finding the course that was used?

He found a website for the school—a private school that had to put itself out there to attract customers. They obviously used professionals to put their website together, or maybe they had a teacher who really knew how to do it. The site was slick and full of news about the achievements of the kids. The four cross-country stars had a page of their own. There were pictures of the four of them as well as a little more of the story. Apparently the boys were not in the lead, in fact, somewhere around half way, they were running as a group around tenth place. Suddenly they found some inspiration and they set off at speed, rapidly overtaking all the other runners. What was particularly interesting to Sam was that as they passed the others they yelled at them to hurry up.

Sam imagined various ways in which he might interview the boys, perhaps go undercover as a reporter, but it was all too complicated. I'd have to fake my credentials and a police report to clear me for talking to children which would be too much, unless it was a real case. Why did these four run so fast, against all their previous form and in the middle of a race that they showed no sign of winning, at least, not until they suddenly found an amazing turn of speed? To Sam, it looked like a familiar pattern. Something scared these boys, so much so that they ran faster than ever before. They must have been trying to get away from something, hence their shouts to the others to hurry up, but why were only these four affected?

As this was going through his mind it struck him that all four boys had blue eyes. Did that matter? Was it unusual? Sam spent a few minutes trying to check back on the other incidents. The young man at the jumble sale had blue eyes, no problem there; he had a criminal record that Sam could check, so there was no doubt about that. What about Dwayne and his brother? After a few moments' thought Sam decided that he had no idea. However, it wouldn't be too hard to see his mother and check on the kids. He made a note.

He thought about Farmer Alsop for a moment but then almost laughed out loud. Alsop was a victim, it was the cows that had been spooked and eye colour probably didn't matter with cows. Working down his list, Mr Sanders was next. He tried to remember talking to him but all he could think about was that it was getting dark by the time he did speak with him and, even if he could remember, the chances were that he might have it wrong. No matter, there was probably a record on the system, thought Sam.

That left the dead gunman, possibly his co-driver and perhaps the two other van drivers. Thinking back over the incidents and all the conversations he'd had, Joyce Prentice's sparkling blue eyes came into his mind. Tick another box. Galvanised by this new inspiration he phoned the morgue—there must be something on the dead gunman.

'Hi, it's Sam Diglis here. I was just following up on something and wondered whether we have a description or an ID for the van passenger yet?'

He listened for a moment and then said to the person at the other end of the line, 'Could you email over what you have? Thanks.'

He picked up the phone and started to dial Maria's number but something stopped his fingers moving. What exactly was he going to say? No, it could wait for the moment. So far out of ten people who he knew had been exposed, six had blue eyes, which was hardly proof. What were the odds? Probably about evens. Blue eyes may not be found in half the population but they were common enough.

Sam checked his email, opened the most recent arrival and read the description of the dead gunman. Eyes: blue. OK seven out of ten. If Dwayne and his brother were added to the list there might be something in it. What could it be about blue eyes that makes a person more susceptible to being influenced by whatever it is?

Hunting around the internet for a few minutes Sam found an article. According to Professor Hans Eiberg in Copenhagen everyone with blue eyes is descended from a common ancestor, somewhere between 6000 and 10,000 years ago. Sam was tempted to email the Professor immediately, just in case he knew something else about blue-eyed people, but he kept coming back to the same question. What exactly was it that caused each of these people to be scared out of their minds?

CHAPTER 19

Boss

The last thing Sam was expecting was a message from the Chief Superintendent asking him to come to a meeting. There was nothing to suggest that it was urgent, or even what it was about; just a cryptic message from a secretary on his answering machine. Look on the bright side, he thought, it gives me a chance to get to the big library.

He phoned, made an appointment and gave it little more thought until he was in the Chief Superintendent's office. He still might find out nothing.

The Chief offered him one of the easy chairs and seemed to be trying hard to be nice, something he had not seen before.

'Everything OK, Sam?'

'I could do without some of it. Three events that produce inquests in one patch generate more paper than I'm used to but it'll pass. Dealing with questions from the widows takes up some time.'

'How many widows?'

'Three. Three too many really but at the moment they seem more interested in asking me for information than using social workers or bereavement counsellors. I've offered them all the usual services but I think the Coroner's Office tends to push them towards me.'

'How's that?'

'They don't get much out of the Coroner's Office. You know the form—nothing until the verdict, can't say anything until that's determined. So, they turn to the nearest official and the local bobby is it. There's not a lot I can say but I have to listen. Local policing goes nowhere if you don't listen.'

The Chief nodded and looked at his notes.

'Has it been getting to you? Do you need a holiday?'

Sam tried hard to keep a straight face. Everyone knew what that meant. Someone, somewhere must have suggested that he wasn't coping.

'No, I'm fine. It'll blow over.' Should he confront it or wait until the boss had finished beating about the bush? He smiled; best wait and see.

'I've been hearing some odd stories.'

'About me?' Sam tried to sound neutral; what the hell could it be? The old bugger was playing around the edges of whatever it was, trying to rattle him.

'What's all this about ley lines, Sam?'

'Ley lines?'

'Ashton and Small said you were going on about them.'

Sam laughed.

'Those two, what a pair! They're capable of getting the wrong end of every stick. They were looking for a way to get some surveillance into Old Stone Farm. I told them it was on a ley line, that bloody great stone at the farm entrance is one of those old stones, like Stonehenge, that sort of age. The farmer the other side of the hill told me all about it, he has one as well. Apparently he had some archaeology boffins studying his, so I suggested to Ashton and Small that they could use that as a cover; have someone muck about near the stone and maybe plant a camera.'

Sam looked to see how this was going down. He went on.

'I'd never heard of it before, so I looked it up a bit.' A hint of a raised eyebrow there. 'You'd be surprised how much baloney is written about these lines.'

'Glad you've spotted that, Sam, uniforms and mysticism don't mix.'

Sam could feel himself freezing. Could the old bastard read minds? This was the clearest warning he could imagine telling him to drop this line of enquiry. Somehow he had to jolt himself out of being frightened. If the old man dropped any more hints like that he might not make it out of the chair. On the wall there was a portrait of old Fitz. Sam found himself staring at it in search of inspiration. Fitz loved a joke, maybe a joke would work.

'So we don't have a Branch that's into that then? I thought we had boffins for everything.' He gave a little laugh and prayed it would be reciprocated.

'Glad you haven't lost you sense of humour, Sam. You weren't playing a joke on Ashton and Small by any chance?'

Sam shrugged his shoulders, feeling the pressure lift.

'I might own up to a tiny bit of playing on their ignorance I suppose. We country coppers have to take what chances we get with the big city boys. Mostly I was trying to help. They seemed to have drawn a blank on getting near that farm. I thought a slightly left field suggestion might jolt them into action. As I understand it, it worked, though it was a bit of a surprise the way it played out.'

'Is that farm on your patch?'

'Just. My boundary is a mile or two past it. I think that's why they asked me.'

'So that'll be another inquest for you?'

'Yes, sir, but fortunately no widows involved.'

Sam knew the tension had passed and relaxed a little. The old man would throw him out now; he must have better things to do.

'Glad you're still on form, Sam. I suppose there's no chance of tempting you back here? '

Sam paused for a moment.

'I think I'm doing a useful job where I am. I'm trying to make policing an important pillar of the community. Just now, with the local vicar being killed and the upset that went with it, I think it's important to stay where I am.'

'Yes, yes, of course, but not closing the door completely?'

'Never close a door that doesn't need closing,' said Sam, pointing at the portrait on the wall behind the Chief.

The boss swivelled around in his chair.

'Keep the nick locked and the cop shop open,' he said. 'Good to know someone remembers the old boy. Keep up the good work, Sam,' he said, swivelling back around. 'Keep up the good work.'

'Thank you, sir,' said Sam and headed for the door. So, he concluded, Ashton and Small have been spreading silly rumours and now there is no way I can involve the office in where this is going. He shut the door behind him and took a deep breath.

I'm on my own now, he thought. I'd better get down to the library and use the opportunity.

CHAPTER 20

Missing

Sam spent the next morning putting a new map on the wall and transferring the pins. The heavy line across the map was conspicuously absent. This might be his home but there was no way he was going to risk being questioned about that line. The boss might think it was crazy but there was something there, something he had to get to the bottom of. On the other hand, with a warning like that there was no point in taking risks.

As he worked, the thought did occur to him that he should have gone for the holiday option, then he could have kept at it in peace. Then again, if he'd said he did need a holiday who knows what else the boss might think he needed?

Help, that's what they would send him. A Community Support Officer or another Constable; someone to get in the way and drive him mad. They'd be junior and they'd rotate them for sure so they could debrief at the other end and make sure Sam wasn't losing it.

Don't be paranoid, he thought. What would you have done in the boss's shoes? A quiet word, always a quiet word, that's the way it went. Subtle stuff but the last thing he needed was a helper, someone he'd have to be responsible for. There was no way he wanted to risk freezing on someone else, especially some kid or a WPC. The whole point of this little niche was to keep away from any of that.

He was almost done when someone knocked at the door. Should he ignore it? One of these days I must get one of those security cameras so I can decide who to let in, he thought. He closed the living room door and opened the front door.

Thoughts of his troubles went out of his mind in an instant; Maria Roberts was standing there looking very distressed.

Before he could even say hello she burst out with, 'Anna's run away.'

'You'd better come in, the place is a bit of a wreck, I'm in the middle of something but it can wait.'

He got her sitting down and picked up a notepad.

'Do you mind if I do this the official way? Why do you think she's missing? What time did you notice and all that sort of stuff?'

Maria pulled a folded piece of paper out of her pocket.

'She left this and I think she packed a bag.'

Sam took the paper "Gone to find someone who can talk to Dad."

'It's her handwriting, I presume?'

'Yes, if anything, trying to be neater than usual.'

'She was at home last night?'

'Yes. She was at home when I went to work too.'

'Which was?'

'About eight this morning.'

'What did she take with her?'

Maria looked distressed for a moment.

'I haven't checked very thoroughly. I'm sure she's taken a rucksack and judging by the things scattered about in her bedroom, she went though her wardrobe deciding what to take.'

'Has she got money? Has she taken credit cards or anything like that?'

'I don't know. She had a holiday job in the summer and I don't think she's spent much of that money. It sounds stupid, I know, but I have no idea.'

'She hasn't gone to your sister?'

'I don't think so, Joyce would have said.'

'I'd better come and look at her room and see if we can find any clues. Is that OK?'

'What about the things you were working on.'

'They can wait.'

'You've changed the map.'

Sam turned to look at the wall.

'Oh, yes.' He thought he'd kept a straight face and was still trying to think whether to explain or to pretend that it needed updating.

'You've taken the line off. Have you given up on that idea?'

She looked at him for a moment.

'No,' she said, 'you haven't. So why change the map?'

'Tricky one that,' said Sam. 'I was called in for a talk with the big boss in the city. He sort of warned me off, said mysticism and uniforms don't mix.'

'Why on earth would he do that?'

Sam knew he must look uncomfortable but her face told him she wasn't going to let it go easily.

'I think some of the other officers were trying to wind me up, or wind him up. Happens all the time. Probably nothing but I thought I'd remove the evidence, just in case.'

'Do they check up on you like that? I never realised.'

'No, they don't. Chances are they'd never see it but the thing about paranoia is you have to do it properly. Now let's go and do something more important. I'll give you a lift home and we can look at Anna's room.'

It looked like the stereotype of any teenager's bedroom, with a little added chaos from the recent packing. Sam set about being systematic, working with Maria to tidy the clothes, looking for anything that might give any indication of where Anna might have gone.

Apart from the note she had left on the kitchen

table, there was nothing else in the room. She had taken her laptop with her.

'Did she use your computer? Might there be anything on there?'

Maria shrugged.

'Maybe, I don't know what she did when I was at work. I think mostly she used her laptop, that's why we bought it, and she's taken that with her.'

'This may sound silly but we need to do a proper description of Anna and decide on a suitable picture.'

Ten minutes later Sam had recorded:

Anna Roberts
Age: 16
Sex: Female
Height: 5ft 2 inches
Weight: 8 stone
Build: Medium,
Eyes: Brown
Hair: Shoulder length, light brown

'OK so far, pity we have no idea what she was wearing. Can you check what jacket or coat she's taken? Outer garments are heavy so she won't have packed several. Did she have a favourite?'

'She has a dark green thing, almost like a camouflage jacket. I can't see that anywhere, so that's the most likely.'

'I should have asked earlier, does she have a phone?'

'She does, but she obviously has it switched off. I've tried it about a hundred times.'

'I think if I was running away I'd switch off to save battery. Send her a text now and then, say you're worried and ask her to text back. If she switches it on for anything else, the text will get through. By the way, did she take a charger with her?' Maria ran upstairs and a minute later was rushing down again clutching a charger.

'Is that a good sign? I mean, does that mean she

wasn't planning to go away for long?'

'How methodical is she? Is that the sort of thing she'd remember?'

'Usually, yes. Sam, can I ask you a silly question?'
Sam grinned.

'Best kind, I've always found.'

'When I said she had brown eyes you had a strange look, almost as though you were relieved or did I miss something?'

'Silly question, silly answer. More than half of the people who seem to have been scared by this thing, whatever it is, have had blue eyes. So far, in all of the cases that I know the eye colour, they had blue eyes. I'm beginning to think that you have to have blue eyes to be susceptible to it. I know it sounds daft but there has to be some explanation for why only some people panic.'

'Who's left on your list?'

'Dwayne and his brother, but not their mum, and Mr Sanders.'

'Joyce has blue eyes.'

'I know, she's already on the list. Now I think about it, the current count is seven out of ten. There may be nothing in it but if it's right then at least it's one less thing to worry about with Anna.'

'Why would that be a worry?'

'If she's off looking for people who can contact spirits, I'd say they'd be dead ringers for a panic attack if they get anywhere near this thing. For all I know they may even be drawn to it. I'm out of my depth here and I'm on my own, the boss made that quite clear, so I'm following every little thing that pops into my head.'

'Are you checking up on the rest?'

'I'm getting Sanders's description sent over; I said I needed it for my files, which is true, sort of. I'll call in on Dwayne's mum, to see how she is.'

'Is there anything else you need here?'

'No, but are you happy if I put Anna's description out? If posters go up it might scare her. I could leave it a day or so right now, it's only been half a day. The note makes it real but she might phone before nightfall.'

Maria nodded, ran her fingers through her hair and was obviously lost in thought for a moment.

'This may seem heartless but it's my way of being pragmatic. It's mostly going to be other people that find her, isn't it? I mean, if she's reported as a missing person, all that stuff goes into action and I'll be sitting here waiting, going out of my mind with worry. There isn't anything practical that I can do; I can't see that rushing around the county looking for her will work. It might help if I had something else to think about. I need something else to do. Is there any chance we could have a look further up that line and see if we can find where this thing started?'

Sam tried to hide his astonishment. Every minute that went by with this woman revealed more depths.

'What about if we see your sister first, before we start putting the word on the wires? Anna may have asked her for advice.'

'I suppose you're right but I don't really want Joyce getting all wound up as well.'

'If I put out a missing person bulletin, she's bound to find out and it would be better if she heard it from you first, wouldn't it?'

She took a deep breath.

'You never know do you? You never know what's going to happen next. One minute, life is good and then wham bang boom, everything is all over the place. I don't feel mad at Anna, I know what she's going through, but Joyce will make it twice as complicated.'

'Anna may have got the idea from Joyce.'

'Yes, Mr Policeman, so she might. Oh hell.' Her face brightened for a moment. 'Actually we can't see

Joyce right now, she's not in, she's having her hair done.'

She looked at him with a mischievous grin. 'We could play hooky for a couple of hours and go and look at your line. Then Joyce would be back and Anna might have phoned or texted.'

'I was thinking that I should spend a bit of time trying to track down mediums and fortune tellers. They have to advertise. They might be mysterious but they can't be invisible, not if they want to stay in business.'

'Sam, we can do that if she doesn't phone this evening.' She paused for a second, fixing him with another searching look. 'Are you sure you're not getting paranoid and wanting to give up on the ley line?'

'Me paranoid? No way.' Some way, he thought, but not the whole way, at least not yet.

'Come on then,' she said, 'we might not get another chance.'

She made it sound like the trip of a lifetime. He gave in.

CHAPTER 21

Up the line

It didn't take Sam long to convince Maria that the motorbike was the best option, and fortunately his spare crash helmet fitted her. This time they used the roads to get to the stone where Sam had talked to the farmer. He took a moment to point out the faint change in soil colour across the field and she could see that it lined up with the top of the barrow, visible against the silhouette of the hill.

From there, it was a short ride to get beyond the next field and on to the Roman road. That ran for almost ten miles before they came to a slight turn which took the main road away from the ley line. A cart track ran in the right direction so they took that. After another mile they stopped. Sam put the bike on the stand and allowed Maria to stretch her legs.

'The vibration's not getting to you?'

'No. It's fun really, it's years since I've been on one of these. It does make conversation difficult though.'

Sam nodded.

'What do you suppose we're looking for?'

'I can't begin to know and to make it more tricky, keep in mind that we're looking for something that happened some time in the past and we don't know how long ago. What's more, the further up this line we go, then the longer ago the events we're after, if that makes any sense.'

'You know, maybe we should have talked to Joyce, she might have come across something that would give us a clue?'

'Only, she's getting her hair done.'

Maria smiled.

'And believe me, that is something that cannot be interrupted. Shall we go on a bit further? This all looks very, very normal here.'

The track led them on for a few miles and then turned abruptly towards a farm a few hundred yards away.

Sam parked the bike and they both looked over the nearby gate.

After a minute, Maria gasped.

'What?'

'You know where this is don't you?'

She looked at him. 'Honestly you should know. You were here when I saw you on TV. I think the cameras were over there.' She said, pointing at the bottom of the field.

'The foot and mouth slaughter.'

'I only saw the TV local report, on both channels. One lot were over there because I think there were some standing about where we are. They interviewed you.'

She swung herself over the gate.

'You were standing here I think and there was all sorts of chaos behind you.' She grinned for a moment. 'You didn't look very comfortable.'

'That's putting it mildly and that interview was after it was all over. You're right, I was here.'

Sam ran his hand through his hair,

'I'd almost forgotten, I think your brain pushes that stuff to the back of your mind. Best not to think about it.'

'What was it really like?'

'I think the papers called it a dark episode. The real problem was everyone was at cross-purposes. The farmer and some of the locals didn't really want the stock killed. I think they regarded the whole thing as unnecessary, so they were dragging their feet.

'The slaughter men weren't really slaughter men. They were marksmen, good with guns, but knew precious little about cows and sheep. I reckon they'd have been OK stalking deer or something, but a whole herd of cattle and a flock of sheep are something else.'

Sam stopped for a moment, lost in his thoughts. He walked forward, shading his eyes as he looked across the field. Maria left him for a few minutes, waiting for the rest of the story.

'Anyone seeing the TV probably didn't realise that it went on for several hours. Once the cows were spooked they kept running and the shooters couldn't get close enough to be sure to shoot them dead in one shot, but they tried anyway. Some of the cows were wounded and running around bleeding. The smell probably panicked the rest. Some got through the hedge over there.'

He pointed at the far side of the field.

'You can still see where they broke through. There were chaps on quad bikes roaring around trying to round them up. There was gun smoke and bike exhaust and a horrible smell of blood and cow dung. It was like something out of hell really. I imagine battlefields are a bit like that. The weather was poor as well, so add a fair bit of mud into the mix.'

He stopped for a moment, turning away from Maria, his hands clenching and fingers intertwining. He walked a few more steps before turning and making his way back to the gate. He leaned on the gate and for a moment rested his head on the top bar.

'Then there were the sheep,' he said, lifting his head to look at Maria again. 'In some ways that was worse. The vet had one of those so-called humane killers, a thing that shoots a bolt into their brains. It works OK on the adult sheep, but it's not so good with lambs. I never understood it really, something about their skulls being soft. You'd think that would make it easier but it's not the way it works. I think some of the lambs were only half dead when they threw them on the pile. They make noises; it sticks in your brain for days afterwards. I lost track of how many animals they killed. Part of the time I had to keep the crowd back, you know, protesters.'

'That's what I saw on TV.'

'Yeah well, maybe it looks better on TV but it's no fun. They were quite right to be protesting but I still had to keep them back. The people the Ministry sent were not helping themselves. I could see the problem, they were trying to control an epidemic, they had a job to do, but I think the vet was from abroad somewhere, taken on to help with the rush of work I suppose. He wasn't used to supervising that sort of operation. He obviously didn't have a plan, or if he did then he didn't explain it well enough. It needed a good plan, needed everyone to know what they were supposed to be doing right from the start. He did try, I'll give him that, but his English wasn't up to it and anyway, the crew they'd given him didn't have any idea either. I don't think any of them had worked together before.

'Once it got out of hand with cows charging about the place, it was quite dangerous. I mean, imagine if some of the folk with placards had been trampled to death. Lord knows where it would have ended. I had my work cut out trying to keep any sort of order. What with the cows trying to get out of the field and some of the placard wavers trying to get in, I hardly knew which way to turn.'

'It must have been awful,' said Maria, taking his hand.

'You know my worst worry? I thought someone might get shot. It would have been just my luck if one of those protesters had broken through and got in the way of a bullet. I tried to tell the shooters to only fire if they could see solid ground behind the animal. Firing up the hill.' He pointed. 'Those rifles have a hell of a range. If they'd shot towards the village, it could have killed some poor sod who'd have had no idea what hit them.'

Maria took both his hands in hers. Slowly, she turned him around, drawing his attention back to the field.

'Where does the line run in the field, Sam? Where exactly?'

Sam studied the map for a few seconds and then walked a few yards into the field, holding his compass. After a few more steps he stopped.

'From here', he said. 'It runs across the field to that bush in the hedge, the slightly darker patch.'

'Next to where you said the cows broke through?'

'Yes.'

'So those cows ran straight along the line and through the hedge?'

'Yes, almost exactly.'

'And where did they kill the sheep?'

'About half way across the field.'

'On the line as well?'

'Now you mention it, yes, almost exactly. What are you thinking?'

Maria walked across the field, stopping almost in the middle and turning around looking in every direction.

'You can't see any sign of it now but there must have been buckets of blood soaking into the soil. It's surprising that it hasn't coloured the ground or changed the grass.'

'I think most it must have been scraped off when they moved the carcasses. They scooped them all up with diggers. They probably scraped off most of the grass and then re-seeded it.'

Maria knelt down and looked closely at the grass,

parting a few blades and feeling the soil.

'What else do you suppose soaked in, Sam?'

'How do you mean?'

'All that fear and terror.'

They both stood, lost in thought for several minutes, until Maria said, 'How good is your mental arithmetic?'

'What?'

'What date was it? Can you work out the time line? I'm thinking this could be it, this thing you're chasing? Did all that terror somehow leak into the ley line and stay alive? I don't know if alive is the right word, but keep going in some way? Herd fear but without the herd. What you've described, and you've been kind and held back a bit, is an awful horror. What you had there was raw fear being herded into a tighter and tighter place, concentrated and kept alive for hours and parked right on top of a ley line. We don't know what ley lines are do we? Are they some ancient property of the earth or are they a leftover from ancient history? Who discovered them? Maybe they don't have energy of their own, maybe they conduct energy, like a wire?

'What happened here was like nothing on earth. When animals get frightened they all pick it up from each other. Herds stampede, like poor Mr Alsop's cows, but when that happens they run, they spread out and the collective fear is dissipated. What happened here was that the fear itself was kept alive for hours on end. Before now I wouldn't have thought of fear as something that could be alive but if you've ever been in a crowd that's out of control then you'll know what it feels like. It's something more than the activity of all the people, it's like an entity with a will of its own.'

Slowly Sam sat on the ground, covering his eyes with his hands for a moment, trying to take himself back there. The noise, the smoke, the smells and the awful anxiety came back. He could feel himself starting to sweat. He opened his eyes and looked at Maria.

'It was beyond anything you'd ever imagine.'

'So they herded fear into a tight pocket and let it live for a while in the dying brains of a couple of hundred animals, some of them very young. Lambs who had no experience of anything, whose brains were raw nervous systems waiting to learn something and then they were filled up with that.

'And they piled it all up on an ancient ley line, a mysterious pathway in the earth, something that was discovered by our ancestors thousands of years ago. Marked out by them with big standing stones—a place to bury dead and a place to remember. Maybe even a place that has memories or holds memories.'

Sam stopped her and taking one of her hands he pulled himself upright. He pulled his notebook out of his pocket and for a few minutes was scribbling on a blank page.

'It's about the right time isn't it?' she said.

He nodded.

'Close enough. Maybe those old folk knew more than we do? What if they found the lines and tried to make damn sure no one went near them? They buried their dead on them, maybe so the spirits had a path to somewhere. Maybe they're roads for spirits to get about? I never thought they made much sense as track ways; sometimes they go straight over hills. A person would walk around but a spirit isn't bothered by gravity. They marked the line with huge stones and what if it all meant KEEP OUT?'

'They may not have been all that clever, Sam. Didn't they make sacrifices from time to time?'

'Maybe they thought the spirits needed company and maybe that was done out of love. One thing's for sure, I bet they didn't think about scaring the wits out of a whole herd of cattle and a flock of sheep and then pouring all that fear into the ground.'

'Look on the bright side, Sam, we don't have to go looking anymore.'

'I wonder if the ones they sacrificed had blue eyes?'

'Don't think about that, Sam, it could have been the other way around. Maybe it was the blue-eyed ones who knew where the lines were.'

'Or maybe the lines are older than blue eyes.'

'Sorry?'

'That research I read said blue eyes only come from a gene mutation some time between 6000 and 10,000 years ago. Maybe the lines are older than that.'

'Go on. I suppose you looked up how old the lines are?'

'Only a bit. You can't tell how old the lines are but some of the stones have been dated. Stonehenge was built around 3500 BC, though it probably took a few hundred years to complete. Carnac in France is another thousand years older than that, but some of the holes at Stonehenge are even older. So, blue eyes developing is in the right time zone. If blue eyes really did come from one individual with a mutation, then it would have taken some time to spread across the world. Maybe the lines only got marked when a blue-eyed person turned up and realised they were there. Maybe that gave them an edge, helped them survive.'

He stopped for a moment, looking around the field. 'Or maybe I'm talking a load of tosh. Trying to guess what happened thousands of years ago is fun but I doubt if it will help much.'

'You mean it won't hold up in court.'

He laughed. For a second he looked at the sky and when he turned back some of the tension had gone.

'There is one blue-eyed person who may help,' said Maria. 'Let's go and find Joyce, she should be back by now.'

It took half an hour to ride back; Sam dropped Maria at Joyce's house and went back to the station.

He'd only been there five minutes when Maria phoned.

'It might help if you came over.'

'On my way.'

When he saw the two of them together, the family likeness was more obvious and Sam found himself wondering how he had missed it when he saw each of them individually. The differences were in their affect. Joyce was more highly strung; somehow both distant and aggressive at the same time. Maria, on the other hand was calm and pragmatic.

'Anna phoned Joyce and asked her to tell me not to worry.'

'When?'

'About twenty minutes ago.'

'Have you checked your phone, is she there as a missed call?'

'No, but she might have tried the phone at home. I haven't got an answering machine so there's no way of telling.'

'What did Anna say?'

'You can listen to it,' said Joyce. 'She phoned while I was at the hairdresser but I've got a machine.'

'That's encouraging.'

'How do you mean?'

'Well, it might be a fair guess that she tried home, got no answer, so phoned her aunty, knowing that there was a machine. It seems like she was trying to make sure you got the message.'

'But she hasn't answered my texts.'

She may still have her phone off. She could have called from a pay phone. Can we listen to it?'

The message was short.

"Hello, Aunty Joyce, it's Anna, you guessed I expect. Can you tell Mum I'm OK, she might be worried. Make sure you tell her today please. Um, I'll ring again, when I have some news. Bye."

Sam listened to it several times, trying to pick out

the background noise as well as any inflection in the voice.

'It's very short so it's hard to be sure about anything. It sounds like a town. I don't think it's a call box in a street or one of those open ones with a hush box, like the bus station. It feels more like a box in a cafe or a hotel. There are some faint voices I think and a car almost at the end. Did you hear anything else?'

The two women shook their heads.

'How did she sound to you, Maria?'

'It's definitely Anna.'

'Sure, but does she sound stressed or nervous?'

'No, not really.' Maria stopped for a moment. 'She almost sounds mischievous, conspiratorial. I didn't think of it until you asked me. I think I was just relieved to hear her voice.'

Sam turned to Joyce. 'What about you, what did you think?'

There was a long pause. Joyce looked at the two of them and then closed her eyes, almost as though she were going somewhere else. A moment later, she was looking down at her lap.

'I don't think I thought anything, only that I was sorry I was out when she called.'

'Did Anna know you were going to the hairdresser today?'

'Yes, I think so. I wonder why she phoned when she did, she should have known I would be out.'

'That may be why she phoned when she did. Let's imagine for the moment that she didn't want to be found but she didn't want you, either of you, to worry. Best thing to do is call when you're out and leave a short message.'

'Hence the conspiratorial tone,' said Maria.

'Possibly.' Sam glanced at Maria and then to Joyce. 'When did she find out about the hairdresser?'

'She didn't need to find out, I always go on the same

day, she'd know that. She's been with me sometimes.'

Sam looked quickly at Maria, one glance told him that checked out.

'Is there something you're not telling us, Joyce?'

Still no eye contact. Sam went on.

'The thing is, in a few hours, or maybe tomorrow, I'll have to put out a missing person report. Technically, she's a minor and a runaway. It sounds to me as though she doesn't plan to stay away long, like she's trying to keep in touch enough that no one starts looking for her. Maybe it would have worked if Maria hadn't already told me she was missing but that puts it in a different category. From what I have so far she could have run away with someone, she could be at risk. I can't just do nothing. If anything happens and I've sat on it then I'm in trouble and the police force as a whole is in trouble and so are you if you've been keeping something back.'

He could see Joyce squirm.

'I think she's told you something, or there's something in the back of your mind. You haven't looked at me, or Maria, for the last five minutes. What is it? What did she say the last time you talked or the time before that?'

Now Maria was beginning to look distressed. Sam made a small movement with his right hand, out of Joyce's eye line but easily visible to Maria. His hand flat, palm downwards, seeming to be pressing down on something invisible. It said "keep calm" in any language.

Sam let the silence work and watched Joyce's face. Eventually she spoke.

'It's all about wanting to talk to John. She kept asking me about it. Every chance she had, whenever Maria was not around.' For the first time she looked up at Maria. 'She knows you don't believe in that sort of thing but what could I do? I gave her some names, told her what to watch out for, how to spot fakes—people who try to con you out of your money. I didn't know she'd run off. Really I didn't.'

'Why didn't you phone me straight away?'

'You were out.'

'On the mobile.'

'I was so shocked, I had to think. I was trying to remember and then you came. I had no idea you'd told the police.'

Sam watched Maria's face. For a moment he thought she was going to say 'it's not the police it's just Sam', but her face said enough.

'I couldn't think what else to do.'

Sam interrupted.

'No harm done. Why don't we quietly work our way through this? She's probably OK, that's what she's telling us, and she doesn't sound as though she's under duress. Let's try to remember some of the names and some of the places she might have gone. With a bit of luck one of them will have seen her and we can go on from there.'

Once the dam was broken it became difficult to stop Joyce talking. For half an hour Sam wrote down names of mediums, fortune-tellers and mystics, sometimes stopping Joyce for more details but mostly trying to make sense of whatever she said about her idea of their strengths and weaknesses. The harder part was trying to put yourself in the mind of a sixteen year old who is heartbroken about her father's death.

Gradually the three of them narrowed it down to a shortlist of people and places to try first. Eventually Sam thought he had enough leads to attack the problem and left Maria to talk to Joyce about their trip earlier in the day. By the time he was ready to go the two sisters seemed close and Sam felt relaxed about the possibility of Joyce wanting to add her own ideas. He was sure he could rely on Maria's pragmatism to keep

Joyce in check.

Sam went back to the station but half an hour later Maria appeared again. She came straight to the point.

'Thanks for taking me with you earlier. I can see what you're doing but are you sure it's wise to go travelling down the ley line?'

'I can't see any other way to check what's there. Looking at maps is OK for villages and towns but it's no good at all for temporary things. There was no clue from the map that a school had a cross-country route right across it. You might spot a school playing field but it depends on when the map was revised. There could be anything that's there one day and gone the next.'

'What sort of thing.'

'I don't know. A pop concert, a fair, a caravan rally, a Boy Scout camp.'

'If you came across something like that what would you do? You can't exactly close it down. You already told me that your boss wouldn't have any of it, why should anyone else?'

'Maria, I can't think what else to do. How could I live with myself if there's another disaster.'

'Then let me come with you.'

For a second he looked surprised.

'Sam, you have blue eyes. Mine are brown, in case you hadn't noticed, wouldn't it be safer if I came with you?'

'Safer for whom? That's exactly why I'm not taking you, or anyone else for that matter. This thing frightens people and they run away from it. If I'm by myself all I can do is run and I can't do any harm to anyone else because there won't be anyone there.'

'At least tell me what part of the line you're planning to walk along. You can't very well tell anyone in the police because you've been warned off looking into this, so tell me. Someone ought to know, Sam, and it seems to me that you're out of options.'

'I don't get why you're doing this. Haven't you got enough to be going on with?'

'Sam, are you completely thick? Let me remind you, the CPS are unlikely to prosecute Mr Sanders because he thought he saw a black car, and even if he did the chances of finding it are slim. That's what you told me and I've checked up as best I can and you're probably right. No doubt I'll get some money from the insurance people, but I bet they'll take ages and they'll pay the least they can get away with so there's not much there that's likely to make me feel good. On the other hand, although I'm no mystic, there may be something in this thing you're chasing and if it is real, then it's what killed John. Without that, the Sanders's would have been away down the road in their flashy car and John and I wouldn't know a thing about them. Nailing this thing is about the only way I'm going to feel better. Now stop making excuses and let's agree how you'll let me know where you are.'

'OK, OK, I'll send you a text. Can you read Ordinance Survey maps?'

'If I work at it.'

'I'll text you a map reference.'

'With your police phone?'

'No, with my private phone. I'll have to take the police one with me, in case I get called, but I'll text you on the other one.'

CHAPTER 22

The coach

The countryside south of Old Stone Farm had a justified reputation for great natural beauty. There were no spectacular hills or gorges but there were some small lakes and a river. The beauty of the region was well recognised as a tourist attraction and the Highways Agency had allowed the construction of a number of small car parks off the road at view points. It was a favourite route for coaches running scenic tours.

Dave Andrews, the coach driver, was explaining that this was a good time of year to see the bend in the river, easily visible from the left hand side of the coach because now that the leaves had fallen and the trees were bare, it was possible to see much more of the water.

Six weeks earlier, parked in almost the same spot, he had been extolling the beauty of the autumnal colours and explaining to his coach tour passengers that because the land was low lying and the river close by, many of the trees held their leaves longer than usual and so the colours here were better than for many miles around.

Put him down on this spot at any time of year and he had a line, a snatch of poetry, a literary reference or some story about a painter that he could twist into being relevant to this place. Much of it had little semblance of truth behind it but it didn't matter. It filled the time between changing into low gear to make the curve into the car park and applying the handbrake and turning off the engine and the microphone. He had to fill one minute and seventeen seconds before the passengers started taking bags off the luggage racks and thinking about their sandwiches.

Dave had done the trip what seemed like a million times. Years ago he had been given a script and since then he had embellished it here and there as a result of questions and things that passengers had said to him from time to time. Two minutes ago he had explained that they would shortly be pulling into a small car park where they could stretch their legs and eat their sandwiches. He wound the wheel around and rolled the coach to a spot he knew would give easy access to the best view and not be too far from the small toilet block, situated discretely behind some evergreens.

He set the brake, stopped the engine and switched off the microphone. He reached for his bag, dug out his thermos flask and had a quick look at the clock as he unscrewed the lid. Bang on time, he thought. Half an hour here, two more views and home for tea.

He couldn't have been more wrong.

The first sign of trouble was a little old lady who felt queer in the toilet. Fortunately, she had a friend with her; at least she didn't collapse on her own and have to be searched for. It was five minutes before the friend came back to the coach to ask for help. By then Mr Terry, another passenger, had slid sideways off his seat and almost fallen into the gangway. Two elderly men were trying to get him back upright, thinking he had fallen asleep. They almost had him in his seat when he yelled and hit one of them. Dave, who had turned to see what was causing the commotion was impressed with the punch. He'd been an amateur boxer in his youth and hadn't seen a straight left as good as that in a long while. It felled the helper in one blow and Mr Terry staggered to his feet and started to run for the door. No doubt some part of his brain had forgotten all about his arthritis, but the joints hadn't. He took two steps and then fell headlong in the gangway and began to shake. Pamela Caulfield, also on the tour and who had been a nurse many years before, was struck by the fact that she'd never seen anyone have a fit and make so much noise at the same time. The screaming certainly got everyone's attention, apart from the helper who was still laid out in the adjoining seat.

The remaining elderly passengers who had been eating their lunch in the seats further back were galvanised into action, but before they got near him it became obvious that he was shouting, 'GET AWAY, GET AWAY.'

That created a dilemma, which had not been resolved in anyone's mind when a quiet woman in the back seat let out a similar yell, stood up too quickly, hit her head on the luggage rack and collapsed in a heap.

Someone took her pulse and Dave heard the dreaded word heart attack. The nearest passenger managed to stretch her out across the back seat and began doing their idea of heart massage.

It was clearly impossible to get from the driving seat to this woman without somehow climbing over the prostrate, still howling, figure in the gangway.

Later, when he was explaining all this to the paramedics, Dave was rather proud of the fact that he had the presence of mind to leap out of the coach and rush to the emergency door at the back and yank it open. That at least got fresh air to the panicking occupants and gave him access to the body flat out in the back seat.

In the luggage compartment there was a portable defibrillator; he'd had the training and he knew he'd have to have a go at it. He vaguely remembered that the machine checked for a pulse before it started blasting off electric shocks, so if the woman had only fainted there was a reasonable chance that he wouldn't make things any worse.

It took a moment for him to wrench open the compartment and grab the machine. It was at about this point that the friend of the woman collapsing in the toilet made it back to the bus. As he turned to go back to the casualty in the back seat he crashed into her, having been unaware while his head was in the luggage compartment that she was coming up behind him. She bounced off, staggered a little, caught her heel on the rough ground and went over backwards to join the squad of horizontal passengers.

Ignoring her for a moment, Dave dashed back to the coach and set about applying the cardiogram leads. As he did so, he noticed that Mr Terry had become ominously quiet. He yelled out, 'If anyone has a mobile phone please call 999, we need at least one ambulance, quick.' That seemed obvious but if he didn't say it for sure someone in the office would have it in for him. He already had visions of headlines about dead passengers and could imagine pictures of himself on the front pages.

He looked quickly at the little screen on the machine and heard a metallic voice saying, 'No pulse, stand clear.'

The machine made a whining noise and then the patient jolted as it delivered a shock. He looked back at the machine. Nothing seemed to have happened. The kit came with a special tube for giving mouth to mouth, so he pulled her head back a little, inserted the tube and blew. Out of the corner of his eye he could see the chest rise. He gave a few more chest compressions and then looked at the machine. There was still no heartbeat. He wondered if he had applied it correctly.

'Has anyone ever worked one of these? Is there a doctor on the coach?' I should have thought of that before, he thought.

A voice behind him said, 'Pamela Caulfield, I was a nurse a long time ago. I think you're doing it right. Has it started her heart?'

'Not so far, well, the machine is working but she's still out cold. Could you have a look at that lady who's collapsed outside, while I have another go here?'

The machine whined and the metallic voice issued its commands. The patient jerked but nothing happened. He did some more chest compressions, blew another lung full of air and hit the button again. There was more whining, and voices, but still no result.

A voice behind him said, 'She's breathing. Pamela says Mrs Nugent has collapsed in the toilet. She was coming to get help when she, um, ran into you.'

'What the hell is going on?'

'Shall I go and see what's happened to Mrs Nugent?'

'Take someone with you. If she's collapsed you won't be able to move her by yourself.'

'Yes, of course. I don't like to say this, but if this woman is hopeless, perhaps you should try the machine on Mr Terry, he's still flat out in the aisle.'

He watched as the small, self possessed figure knelt by the woman on the floor of the car park, said something to her, and then called through the door.

'Two strong men please.' She set off across the car park, barely sparing a glance at the two men getting out of the bus to follow her. I bet she was a Matron, or at least a Ward Sister, he thought as he pumped more air into the woman in front of him. He watched as the machine did its thing again, still with no result. A quick look at the dials told him that it had given its maximum shock, so he unstuck the leads, climbed over the seat and set about trying to attach the wires to the man on the floor.

The one former helper who was still upright was tending to the passenger who had been punched.

'Is he alive?' Dave asked.

'He has a pulse and he's breathing. I don't think he needs that thing. Just mind out if that chap on the floor wakes up.'

It took a few seconds to apply the leads to Mr Terry and set the machine going. He listened to the familiar sounds and wondered how long the battery lasted. The body on the floor jolted, but there was no result. Dave did some cardiac massage, blew some air and tried the machine repeatedly.

He had got nowhere by the time the ambulance arrived and the battery had died. He sent the paramedics to the toilet block to find out what had happened to the group over there, while he climbed out on to the car park and was very pleased to find he could talk to the lady he had knocked over, who was now sitting up talking to a friend.

A few minutes later the ambulance men reappeared, along with three figures that were walking alongside a stretcher. Ms Caulfield led the party but their body language told him that the woman was dead. The newspaper headlines in his brain changed from "two tragic deaths on coach trip", to "three die in tragic coach mystery".

The paramedics called another ambulance and tended to the two living casualties until it arrived. They were taken to the hospital and the three bodies to the morgue.

The police had been called and by then had taken identification details from the remaining passengers. Dave, meanwhile, had called his office and managed to get across that he was in no fit state to drive the coach back. Another driver was brought out by taxi and eventually the coach made its way back to the depot, where relatives and staff from the various old people's homes were waiting to help the passengers.

The next morning there was, as expected, a headline and photographs in the local newspaper. "Pensioners die on tragic bus tour". There was not a picture of the driver, though he was mentioned. In the end it was exhospital Matron Pamela Caulfield who got most of the attention. She praised the driver's efforts, pointed out that many of the passengers had multiple diseases and were known to have weak hearts. Ms Caulfield described in some detail the benefits of the portable defibrillator and said she wished such things had been available when she was working. The reporter did point out that none of those treated with it survived but it didn't get him very far. The important thing, she observed, was that they knew for sure that the patients were dead. That was tragic but it allowed those who were available to concentrate their efforts on the casualties who could be saved. The reporter gave up at that point; somehow, he could not summon the nerve to ask which hospital she had worked at. She might look old but there was no doubt in his mind that she had a few more lectures in her and he had no desire to be on the receiving end of another one.

CHAPTER 23

Nightmare

Sam Diglis woke in a cold sweat. He had a routine to handle this—get out of bed, visit the bathroom, pee, towel off the sweat, turn the duvet over so that the sweat can evaporate and go back to bed.

It had worked a hundred times before, not that he kept count, not any longer. He had counted, back when it first started, back when he was seeing the psychologist. Back then he would get out of bed and write down the details of the nightmare, those that he could remember. He kept records for a year and a fat lot of good it did.

'I think it keeps me awake,' he'd said to the shrink. 'By the time I've made notes, I'm wide awake. I end up having a drink, wondering around in the dark, crashing into the furniture as often as not and it takes forever to get back to sleep.'

'You could put the light on,' she said.

'That makes me even more awake.'

'But how do you take notes in the dark?'

'The computer's bright enough and sometimes I use the tape recorder.'

Eventually he'd had enough of those conversations and thought he'd try not writing and not recording and then he'd worked out the current routine. Sam thought it was better, felt pleased that he'd worked it out for himself and stopped seeing the shrink. These days, when he remembered, he'd make a cross on the calendar in the morning; that was enough of a record. A year back, after a couple of bad nights, he'd actually gone back and checked. The frequency was definitely going down and he'd checked again two months ago and it looked better still.

Now that Sam was awake this time, he said to himself, stick to the routine, it was only one thirty, plenty of time for a decent sleep.

He was still in that fuzzy zone between sleep and wide awake when it came at him again. In the past there was something familiar about the nightmare. The shrink never really understood it. It should have been the man with the gun or bullets flying by, but it was never like that. The one common factor was the freezing. Sam motionless and something coming at him. In the days when he'd tried to record everything he'd been amazed at the number of hazardous situations his brain could dream up. Dream up, that was the crucial phrase, because when he was wide awake none of these things ever crossed his mind.

In his dreams he'd been engulfed by avalanches, landslides, falling buildings, runaway trains. It was always something coming at him and he could not move. There was almost no end to the ways that something could fall on a person. He'd have a delightful dream about being in an amateur dramatic performance. He'd be enmeshed in the drama, interacting with the other actors and somehow being in the part and enjoying the show all at once, and then the scenery would fall on him. It never hit anyone else and there was always that heart-stopping moment when he could see it coming and he froze.

It woke him, of course; he never died in his dream, right there in the bed. He always woke and one way or another there was the cold sweat routine.

Now, he sat bolt upright in bed and this time he turned on the light. He tried to recall what had come at him. He got out of bed, walked around for a while and eventually went downstairs. He poured half a glass of milk from the fridge and drank it slowly. Something had come at him but it was black and shapeless. He stared at the map, almost put a pin in his own house but then stopped.

'This isn't real,' he said to himself. 'I need a map of what's inside my head.'

As he made his way back upstairs he knew his brain was inventing what it thought the various victims had seen. Interesting, he thought, and there's only one way I'll ever find out if my subconscious has got it right.

He fell asleep again with his mind imagining ways of being able to record his brainwaves so that he could play the dreams back while he was wide awake. He almost woke himself up again as the thought crossed his mind that he was keeping his head very still to avoid disturbing the imaginary electrodes that he had mentally attached to his skull.

It was three a.m. when the next attack came. This time he didn't really wake. He was awake, or at least dreaming that he was awake, and being enveloped by blackness. It had come at him very fast, out of nowhere, and everyone around him in the dream had run. Sam stood alone, frozen to the spot and everything that had been around him disappeared into the blackness. For a few seconds he could hear the retreating footsteps of the people running. The sounds faded, the screams died away and the ebony darkness descended.

Inside the dark he tried to feel the ground but there was nothing there. That's because I'm in bed another voice seemed to say.

So why can't I feel the bed?

The blackness felt tangible, not suffocating, not really touching him, but somehow containing everything. He had no body, there was just him. Somewhere in the void there was the idea of Sam Diglis, the bit that was left if you took away all the blood and bones and skin and fingernails.

If I smile will my teeth look white?

You have no teeth, another voice said.

Where's my body?

It got up and left half an hour ago, it's making tea and toast in the kitchen.

Not without me, he thought and woke up laughing.

He got out of bed, surprised to find that this time there was no sweat, and set off for the kitchen again.

He looked at the clock and it was four thirty. He picked up the kettle and his hand jerked back from the hot metal, or so he thought. It took him a second to realise that the kettle was cold not hot. It was hot in my mind, he thought. Bloody convincing too. Am I really awake? He walked through to the back door, stepped outside and looked at the moon. In a few seconds he was shivering. OK, so probably I'm awake, or very good at dreaming. How can you tell if you're awake?

He closed the door, went back inside and sat down to make notes. It was half an hour before he had stopped writing and decided to risk going back to bed. As he fell asleep for the third time that night a new thought hit him.

Everyone else in the last dream ran and I froze and the thing stayed with me. That's got to be a decent plan, he thought. If I can find it, it'll attack me and I'll be scared out of my mind and I'll freeze. That's my secret weapon. If I'm standing there I won't be able to move and it'll be trapped out of the ley line, out of the ground.

That's too good an idea to risk forgetting he thought, as he dragged himself out of bed yet again and wrote it down.

By five o'clock he was asleep and was woken by the alarm two hours later.

Over breakfast he read his notes and then the morning paper. Sam read the report about the coach, plotted the position of the car park on the map, did the calculations three times to be certain and finished his breakfast, muttering, 'I bet I know what colour eyes the victims had.'

He called the pathology lab, whose assistant he was getting to know well by now, and by lunch time he had confirmation—all three victims had indeed had blue eyes.

CHAPTER 24

Anna

Anna took the bus into town. She had done that many times, so there was nothing new or daring involved. From the bus station she made her way on foot to a part of town that she'd never visited before. As she walked down strange streets, wherever she looked she saw unfamiliar sights and each new image carried a small dose of anxiety with it. By the time she'd reached the old factory building, she knew she was wound up and needed a moment or two to take stock.

She had no idea what they used to make in the massive Victorian building, no doubt some product that could be shipped out across the vast British Empire of the time. Now it was an anonymous edifice of red bricks. Inside, someone must have had a government grant, or something like it, to establish studios for arts and crafts. The refurbishment had obviously been done on a shoestring and a piece at a time, unless the variation in decor and structure was some kind of art project itself. In many places the old industrial heritage showed through. Concrete floors, strange pieces of ironwork attached to the walls indicating some long lost function and ceilings too high to make heating economical. Parts of the building had been converted—small studios and offices had been constructed, mostly from breeze-block, or in some cases partition walls made of wood. They varied enormously in size and activity, though many were simply shut.

She strolled down a wide corridor, between the

studios, taking a moment to watch a potter making a huge vase. She watched the structure rise under his hands and then change shape as one arm disappeared beyond the elbow deep inside, while the other carefully steadied the clay on the outside. After a while the wheel slowed and stopped and the two hands stretched part of the rim and the vase became a jug. She was tempted to wait and see the handle attached but the potter left it for a while, stood back to gaze at it and then moved further back into the studio to pick up a drink.

Anna moved on, past some gorgeous textiles, an array of paintings and a room full of fascinating woodcarvings, until she found the cafe. She was a little surprised to discover that it was waiter service; somehow, it was easier to simply stand at a counter and point at what you wanted. She tried to look as though she did this all the time; sat down and studied the menu.

What did modern young women consume in the middle of the morning? She had no idea. A coffee seemed safe enough but what to have with it? Right now she felt too nervous to be hungry, but she ought to have something, if only to look normal. She glanced around the room, trying to match what she could see on people's plates with the words on the menu. Why do cafes call things by such fancy names? She couldn't very well point at someone else's plate and say I'll have that. She was on the point of picking something at random when the waitress turned up.

Before Anna could speak, the waitress had launched into a short sales pitch including something about a special range of cakes cooked on the premises. Anna ordered a coffee and one of the specials. Maybe that's why they have them, she thought, or perhaps it's a rip off and they make more money on those items. Never mind. What she needed was a little peace and not to feel as though she stuck out as a runaway teenager. She shoved her rucksack further under the table and put all her attention into examining the leaflet she'd picked up at the door. There was a plan of the whole building on the back. After a few seconds she found the place she was looking for.

She still had her finger on it and while she searched in her bag for a pencil, the waitress came back.

'Oh, she's very good,' said the waitress, whose badge informed the world that her name was Sally.

'Have you been to her?'

'Not myself, love, but plenty of customers do. Some of them are in here all the time.'

This could be a set up, thought Anna, a sales pitch. She tried to smile.

'She's not your sister is she?'

Sally laughed.

'No. No, love, she's not from round here. No one in our family is exotic like that but all the ladies swear by her.'

Anna left it at that. She tried to drink her coffee slowly and eat her cake as elegantly as she could, her stomach fluttering with nerves. The short exchange with Sally had, if anything, made it worse but maybe the sugar in the cake would help. At least she wouldn't feel hungry.

Twenty minutes later she felt steady enough to leave the cafe and head for the right part of the building. As she turned the last corner she saw the shop.

She had no idea what to expect and therefore anything might have been a surprise. The window display was obviously designed to convince almost anyone who was seeking a fortune-teller that what they sought was indeed inside. There were zodiac signs, planets, crystal balls and any amount of mystic looking paraphernalia. Fortune telling was not exactly what Anna had in mind, but someone who could connect with the future might also connect with the dead.

The door opened into a small shop that also served as a waiting room. There were chairs, a low table and some magazines. On the counter was a bell, alongside a crystal ball. Anna rang the bell and looked into the ball. In the back of her mind she half expected it to be some sort of video device so that when she rang the bell, she would see a face appear in the ball. Nothing happened, but half a minute later a woman appeared.

The woman was dressed completely in black—not a Goth sort of dress covered with lace and metal decorations, but a matt black that reflected no light, so in the dim at the rear of the shop it was actually hard to tell what she was wearing. It might have been a sweater and bell-bottom slacks or it might have been a one-piece jumpsuit or even a long flowing dress.

Her voice had a trace of a sort of middle European accent. She could have been from Poland or Hungary or perhaps a genuine Gipsy, or maybe the accent was an act.

'I can help you how?' she asked.

Anna had rehearsed this in her mind a hundred times but now that the moment had arrived it was hard to get it right.

'It's about my dad.'

'You wish to find who your father is?'

'Oh no, I need to talk to him.'

'And for this you need my help? Is he far away, is he not known to you?'

'He's dead.'

There was a long silence until she said, 'Ah, I see. Come.' She led the way into a room at the back of the shop. As she opened the door she touched a button on the wall that was barely visible. The touch of her hand was so quick that most people would have missed it in the dim light. A sign appeared by the door that said "engaged, please wait". That's cool, thought Anna, almost like she did it with mind control.

The second room had a table in the middle with some simple chairs around it. There was hardly any light. The woman in black flicked a switch and the lights came up a bit.

'Sit down, tell me about this. He has been dead a long time, yes?'

'No, a few weeks ago, it feels like yesterday. He was killed by a car while he was walking our dog.'

'And why you wish to talk to him?'

'There are too many things I wish I'd said, things I was going to tell him, only there wasn't time.' Anna stopped for a moment, looking at her hands resting on the table. She could see her fists clenching, almost of their own free will.

'I wanted to say sorry.'

'Sorry? For what, sorry?'

'I should have been walking the dog. It was my idea, getting a dog and I promised I'd walk him.' Her voice trailed off into a whisper. 'I promised.'

Anna looked up quickly as the woman took her hands and held them in silence for a minute.

'Have you talked to your mother about this?'

'I can't.'

For a moment there was a question in Madame Black's eyes and then a half smile crept across her face.

'Your mother is too upset herself, you are afraid to hurt her more, this is a barrier between you. Yes?'

'Yes.' Anna glanced for a moment at Madame's face and instantly looked away from the penetrating glance. 'I hear her crying at night. She's very brave. She's still working, I think that's how she survives.'

Madame continued to hold Anna's hand, slowly bringing them together and wrapping them in a gentle caring embrace.

'I can't help you,' she said. 'I wish I could. If I could, I would.' The accent had faded. 'I could take your money and tell you platitudinous nonsense and very likely fool you into thinking you could talk to your dad through me but it wouldn't be right, and it probably wouldn't help.'

Anna felt a slight squeeze on her hands, the accent had gone and she sounded more like a teacher than a fortune teller.

'It wouldn't be right. You need to know that most people in this business can't help you. Don't waste your money, your time or your hopes. Most of them are like me. They can read what people want and give them something like it. That is not what you need. There is only one person I know who has a talent that might come close to what you are searching for. I can't guarantee that she'll even see you or help but it may be worth a try.'

There was another squeeze and as Anna looked up Madame let go, stood up and walked quickly across the room. In a moment, she was back with a small leaflet.

'She works with this travelling fairground. You are in luck because they are not far away. You could get there tonight if you're quick.'

The woman glanced at Anna's face.

'Get a taxi with the money you would have given me.' The woman stood and conducted Anna to the door. 'Go quickly and my time not waste any more.' The accent was back. It's for show in case anyone is listening thought Anna. She turned to thank the woman but she was already turning to walk back into the shop. Anna was left with the tiniest hint of a kindly smile as the door closed.

She walked back to the bus station, partly to steady her nerves but also because she knew there was a taxi rank there. If the taxis were parked, she thought, it would be safe enough to ask how much the journey would cost. If she hailed a cab in the street they might not take kindly to some kid wanting to negotiate.

The price was less than she expected but it seemed

as though the fair was miles out in the country. When they got there no one could have missed it. Hundreds of cars were parked and there were thousands of people milling around.

The thumping music and the general excitement carried Anna along. This time she had no map, no way of knowing where anything was, so she had no alternative but to try to work her way around the whole place until she found the stall. She had a name and the woman in black had warned her not to be put off by the external appearances. "It may look cheap and tacky," she'd said, "and be full of mystic rubbish but take no notice, that's just fairground stuff; the woman has talent, that's all that matters."

That thought, and the push of the crowd, carried Anna along. She'd been shuffling, avoiding trouble for twenty minutes before she began to feel anxious again. She thought about her mum and Aunty Joyce whenever there was a lull in the crush. She wished she'd been able to tell them but they'd only have laughed at the idea. She kept her phone off and left it in her deepest pocket; the last thing she needed was for someone to steal it. That was her way home if things didn't work out.

She was so lost in these thoughts that she almost missed the tent. When she saw it she had to laugh for a moment. Someone had tried to think of every stereotype of a gypsy fortune-teller that anyone, of any age, might have in the back of their mind and somehow they had assembled all those images into a tent.

The background colour was black but every kind of star and magic sign that you could imagine was sewn on at every angle. There was even a rainbow with a pot of gold and a small creature, who might have been a leprechaun, standing guard over it. Important not to lose the Irish trade, she thought.

She waited outside for a couple of minutes to see if anyone came out. The crowd continued to file past and the music thumped away in the background. I hope the tent deadens the sound a bit, she thought, or I'll never hear a word this woman says.

Eventually she screwed up her courage and went in.

Like the outside of the tent, the inside could have been taken from a fairy tale, or more likely half a dozen tales. There was a woman sitting at a small table. She wore a grey dress with a shawl that almost covered her face. Inevitably, there was a crystal ball in front of her.

Anna sat down and waited to see what happened.

'What do you seek from Gina?' She had the same slightly accented speech as the woman from the shop.

'Madame Black sent me to you. My father was killed recently and there are things I wish I'd had time to tell him.' The words came out in a rush and Anna almost burst into tears. Clutching the sides of the chair and staring at the floor, she waited for a response.

She felt a movement opposite her but didn't dare to move.

'Look at me, child, look at me.'

Anna held her breath and with a great effort raised her head and looked across the table to find two calm blue eyes examining every inch of her face. Hardly daring to breath and riveted by the woman's gaze she heard her say, 'Give me your hands.'

Anna reached across the table and felt her fingers being wrapped in a warm gentle grip. Slowly the woman closed her eyes.

'Think now only about your father; nothing else, just father. Of him and only him, think.'

After half a minute the blue eyes opened again and she released her grip.

'I may be able to help but time it will take. Quiet it will need and peace it will need. There is no peace here now. Too much confusion and noise there is.'

'I can wait,' said Anna.

'You can wait because you have run away to find me. But Gina asks herself, how long can this girl wait?'

'As long as I need to.'

The woman laughed.

'No, into trouble you will get me. A runaway I cannot harbour.'

'The fair is open all night, I can stay at the fair.'

'And in the morning, so tired you will be, that I will not be able to help you.'

She looked at Anna again, smiled and suppressed a chuckle.

'Young people these days are impossible,' she said in a perfect Southern Counties accent. 'I suppose there is a sleeping bag in that rucksack?'

Anna nodded, then grinned.

'Do you have to talk like Yoda?'

'Is it that bad? Never mind, go and get some food. You'll find places to eat around the fair. They're safe enough. Enjoy the fair. You can sleep in my caravan and you can help me this evening and tomorrow. You can earn what you should be paying me by doing chores and I'll see what I can do. Have you told your mother you're safe?'

'Um, sort of.'

'I see. Sort of is not enough. Do it properly, she'll be worried. She doesn't deserve that if her man has been killed.'

Anna burst into tears.

'Tell your mother you are alive and safe. You don't have to say where you are, there'll be time enough for that tomorrow.'

CHAPTER 25

The Fair

Try as he might, Sam could not stop thinking about the coach. The vehicle had obviously been moved and the casualties all taken to hospital, but he wanted to see the site. Once he had cleared up routine work he made the short trip, parked where the bus had stopped and took his compass bearings. The ley line ran diagonally across the area where coaches parked and the toilet block was right on the line, 50 yards away.

He stood in the open, trying to be as close as he could to the line, trying to let his mind be as open as possible. Nothing happened. It's moved on, he thought.

He looked at the map again and worked out how to navigate to the next point where a road crossed the line. As he turned towards the car he caught sight of a small poster stuck on the gateway into the car park. It didn't convey much information beyond the fact that there was a fair, staying for a week, and not far down the road. Sam took a picture of the poster, folded up his map and set off towards the fair.

It was easy enough to find, they hardly needed to advertise—you could see the helter-skelter tower from a mile away.

Sam parked and consulted his map, taking a moment to make a rough calculation of the time line. If it was at the coach park yesterday then it will get here some time tomorrow. He put the pad down, muttering 'bloody hell' and set off to explore. He allowed himself the luxury of strolling around; fortunately he was not in uniform. At this time of morning there were no crowds and many of the stalls were closed. He enquired at a few of the ones that were open and soon established that within an hour or so everything would be running. He found a quiet corner and consulted his map again; there was no doubt that the fair was very close to the line. If ley lines really were only a few yards wide, then only two or three attractions were directly on it. How many people might be affected would depend on how sensitive they were.

The other question was when. He had calculated the progress of the thing down the line but it was hard to be precise, the fair covered a hundred yards or more; it might take several hours for the thing to move through that distance. It's going to turn up this afternoon and trouble could break out at any point. On the other hand, if I'm a bit out it might not get deep into the fair till the middle of the night. Please let it be the middle of the night, he thought.

He found a stall that was selling drinks and bought a paper cup of tea. Clutching that and occasionally taking a sip, he walked through the whole fair, trying to think what to do. He couldn't stay all day and even if he did, what could he do? If the thing got into someone's head, what might happen? There might be a fight or some sort of general rush for the car park. Surely the people who ran the fair must be used to drunks and rowdy behaviour; they could probably handle it. On the other hand, a stall keeper might succumb or a man running one of the rides. That could be nasty.

He finished his tea and was looking for a waste bin when he caught sight of a girl walking between the caravans behind the fair. She was carrying a rubbish bag, obviously clearing up after last night, but there was something very familiar about her. She had gone out of sight before he realised it could be Anna. He tried to follow but by the time he'd moved to a position where he could see clearly there was no sign of her. He looked at his watch, the missing person bulletin would probably go out this afternoon. If he could find Anna before then it would save a heap of trouble.

Why would she be here? It made no sense. How could the fair have anything to do with searching for a way to talk to her dad, unless that was a ruse. Maybe she just wanted to have fun. He walked back to the main aisle and examined all the attractions more carefully. He found one where the woman tending it looked approachable. He might have to buy a toffee apple but there were worse things in the world.

He approached the stall, looked at the merchandise and waited for the sales pitch to begin. Once he had his money out and she was sure of a sale, he changed the subject.

'You've got a good range of things here, do you have a fortune teller or a psychic?'

'Just the one, love, but she won't start until after lunch. Tent in the second aisle, can't miss it, covered in stars and such. She's very good but you've got a few hours to kill before she's open.'

He took a bite out of the apple, smiled and headed for the other aisle. It took two minutes to find the tent. He thought about making enquiries there and then but the sign said "closed". He then doubled back to the car. In a minute, he was on the road and phoning Maria.

'I think I might be on to something. I've been to a fair further down the line. I thought I saw Anna. If I pick you up can you come with me after lunch.'

There was a long pause.

'I'll have to get someone to cover for me. I'll have to ring you back. Are you staying there looking for Anna?'

'No, I'm heading back. I've got things to do but I think I know why she's here and if I'm right she'll still be here this afternoon. Try to get free if you can.'

***

As Sam was leaving, Anna was finishing the chores she had been given. She had remonstrated with Gina, saying that she had the money to pay, but Gina would have none of it. She insisted that she needed to see Anna doing normal things, being herself, to help her find the right wavelength.

Anna had been suspicious at first. Gina's patter sounded like the fake mediums she had read about, people who were good at picking up details that they later wove into predictions, telling the client what they desperately wanted to know. After a night's sleep and some work around the fair Anna felt more confident and began to express some doubts.

Gina was disarming.

'Oh, I know what you mean, I can certainly do that but that's no use to you. Listen girl, I have a little bit of talent, a tiny bit. It doesn't work every time so don't get your hopes too high, but if the right things click I might be able to give you something. Just relax and we'll do it my way. Did you phone your mother?'

Anna shuffled her feet and looked at the floor.

'Sort of.'

'Meaning?'

'I sent her a text. She'd sent me a load while my phone was off so I texted her back.'

'Were there any missed calls?'

'Three, I think.'

Gina grimaced.

'So we know she cares about you and she's worried. She's not going to stop worrying because she's had one text, is she?'

'I suppose not.'

Gina sighed.

'We'll talk after lunch. See if you can manage to talk to your mum this morning, you can ask her to come if you like.'

She looked at Anna again with those piercing blue

eyes.

'Oh I get it, you want to do this yourself.'

Anna was on the point of tears again.

'It's not that. It's just that Mum doesn't think it's possible; she's very practical. My Aunty Joyce used to be into spirits and stuff, that's where I got Madame Black's address from, but Mum doesn't believe in anything like that.'

'So why didn't you come with your aunty?'

'It's not that simple. Her husband was killed as well.'

'In the same accident?'

'No, another one.'

Gina put her arm round her and for a few seconds stood and held her.

'After lunch, then... I'll do the best I can.'

Two hours later Anna sat in the chair opposite the crystal ball. She looked into it, moving her head around, trying to see something inside.

'Do people see things in there?'

'They see what they want to see. Don't bother about that.'

Gina pushed the ball to one side.

'Give me your hands and relax.'

Anna stretched her hands across the table and felt Gina's warm grip.

'It takes time, just relax as much as you can.'

Anna leaned further forward and then, finding the stretch slightly uncomfortable, laid her head on the table, turning it to one side and allowing her shoulders to droop so that she was looking sideways on, into the depth of the tent the other side of the crystal ball. She closed her eyes and tried to think of her dad.

Images of the last time she'd seen him flashed through her mind. The half open door, looking up from her books, a raised eyebrow that she knew meant he was asking if she was going to walk the dog. It seemed such a trivial question, and she was working. If he'd come when she needed a break, when she was bogged down in a boring bit, it might all have been different.

Try as she might she couldn't get past that kindly look—the acceptance that he could do something for her, out of consideration, out of pleasure because she was so obviously embedded in her homework, and that had to be a good thing. She could see it all in his face.

'Don't worry, I'll go.' The door had closed and that was the last thing he ever said to her. Ever.

She could feel tears running down her cheeks. Was that all right; did that spoil anything, would it work if she was crying?

She didn't dare ask. The warm grip continued so she let the tears run; she couldn't break free to get a tissue.

"Don't worry, I'll go." Where, she thought, where did he go? That was what this was all about, finding where he'd gone.

Then something changed, the grip got tighter, much tighter. Anna held on in suspense. Was this the moment, was this where Gina got through? How did it work, did her dad's voice come through Gina, did Gina hear her dad and then relay what he said? Should she speak? If she, Anna, spoke, did Dad hear? The questions flooded into her mind, almost breaking her concentration.

Think about Dad; try to keep thinking about Dad.

The grip became so tight that her hands hurt and she could not think about anything else. Reluctantly she looked up, lifting her head from the table and forcing herself to sit upright to look at Gina.

The blue eyes were wide open, staring, terrified and her breathing was coming in short gasps, the muscles on her neck standing out like taught ropes. As she watched, Anna saw Gina's colour change from deathly pale to a dark pink and beads of sweat broke out on her forehead as though she'd been running for miles. Her whole body was tense and her grip more and more painful.

This can't be right, Anna thought. Talking to my dad can't be this scary. Slowly, somehow not wanting to break the spell, she worked one hand loose from the grip, her skin burning as she dragged her left hand free. One by one she peeled Gina's fingers from her other hand. As she freed the grip from her own hand, each finger curled into a tight ball, the nails digging into Gina's palm.

What to do? Anna called out. 'Gina, what's the matter?' There was no answer, not a blink of recognition. Is she having a fit, she thought? What did Mum say about how to treat people with fits? Keep them breathing and don't let them hurt themselves. Wait until it stops.

If only Mum was here, she'd know what to do.

What if she's having a heart attack, what does that look like? Gingerly Anna tried to find a pulse, feeling around the wrist in front of her. Gina's muscles were so rigid, her fists so tightly clenched, that it was hopeless. Anna pushed her chair backwards and stood up. In two steps she was at the other side of the table. You can feel the pulse in the neck, Mum had shown her once. Where was it?

Trying to ignore how strange it felt to be putting her hands around someone's neck, she tried to find a heartbeat somewhere between the taught muscles. Eventually there was a fluttering rhythm under her fingers. That must be it, she thought. She daren't let go now that she'd found it, but she couldn't time it unless she could see her watch. Keeping one hand on the pulse, Anna tried to pull her sleeve up to see her watch, pushing her arm against her side, trying to get enough friction, but it slid back down.

Did Gina have a watch? Keeping her right hand on

the pulse, Anna reached across and pulled Gina's sleeve up to her elbow. As she did, she could feel the tense muscles under the skin; they felt like steel hawsers but there was a watch and it had a second hand.

Desperately trying to concentrate, and ignoring the grunting breathing alongside her ear, she counted. After fifteen seconds she stopped, but found she could not think how to calculate the pulse rate by multiplying by four. Every number that came into her head seemed far too high. The pulse is supposed to be seventy something but she kept getting numbers way beyond that.

She counted again, this time for a whole minute. At least that was easy to do; start when the second hand got to twelve and wait until it got there again. Really, you could begin anywhere, she thought, but I'll never be able to remember where I started. She waited until the hand moved around and then counted as though her life depended on it; one hundred and ninety.

She felt relieved and scared at the same time. Somehow knowing that her multiplication had been right was reassuring but surely no one was supposed to have a pulse that fast. She wished she'd listened to Mum more often; all that boring stuff about nursing had a point after all.

Gina was breathing. That must be good. What was all the stuff she was supposed to have learned? Airway, breathing, circulation. Airway? There must be one because Gina was breathing, but her teeth were clenched tight. She felt Gina's jaw muscles. There was no way she could get her mouth open, it would have to do. Gina had a pulse; OK, but way too fast.

What about a stroke? What did that advert say? FAST, but what did it stand for? "F" is for face, that was the first bit. She was symmetrical, no sign of her face dropping or one arm or leg being paralysed. The "A" is for arm. OK, so far so good. What's the "S"—

speech? Impossible to say and why was Gina so completely tense; she looked as though she was rigid with fear. What's the "T" for? It can't be terror. Time, that's it, time. I've got to do something quickly. Anna found herself faced with the inevitable dilemma of every first aider—should she run for help and risk abandoning the person in front of her or stay, but not know what to do if things got worse?

Yelling for help seemed like a good idea, though with fairground music pounding outside that didn't seem to offer much help. If only Mum was here.

She yelled,

'HELP,' as loud as she could and her Mum appeared.

Anna almost passed out. Was she dreaming? What was going on? Was this magic?

Was she imagining her mother because she was so desperate? She reached out a hand to touch Maria and was even more amazed to feel solid flesh.

'Mum. How?'

'Sam Diglis saw you and phoned me. I couldn't get off until now. Who is this?'

'Gina the gypsy, she's a sort of fortune-teller. She's a very kind lady but something terrible is happening. Her breathing is wrong, her pulse is a hundred and ninety and she seems to be terrified. She was supposed to be talking to Dad for me. Mum, what have I done?'

Maria was already feeling Gina's pulse and moving alongside her. She took a torch out of her pocket and flashed it in each of the blue, staring eyes. Both pupils were widely dilated but reacted to light.

'It's not you, love, I'll explain later. I'm trying to think what to do.'

Maria held Gina's wrist, feeling her pulse again.

'It's more than a fast pulse, it feels like her pressure is sky high too. We need to get her to hospital. Have they got a first aid station here?'

'Yes it's along the aisle, at the back.'

'OK, go and see if they have a wheelchair and get them to call an ambulance.'

Anna ran and Maria turned back to Gina.

'I know what it is,' she said as close to an ear as she could get. 'Try to be calm, try to breathe deeply. It can't kill you.' At least I hope it can't, she thought. 'It's afraid. It's a spirit that's afraid, try to let it pass through.'

The tent door burst open and Anna pushed a wheelchair through.

'The man can't come, he's dealing with someone who's bleeding.'

'What about an ambulance?'

'He said I could call one myself but he said they take ages to come from town. I couldn't really say what was the matter so I said she was having a sort of fit.'

'Not a bad guess. Now here's a problem for you. This lady, does she have any potions or stuff like that? What I could really do with is strong camomile tea.'

Anna beamed.

'She has some in her caravan.'

'I won't ask how you know. Help me get her into this chair and then go and make some, as quick as you can and make it strong.'

'Where are you going to take her?

'Along the aisle to the left, as far as I can go. A hundred yards that way if I can get that far.'

'The field goes on more than that. Does she need fresh air or something?'

Maria picked up the table and heaved it across the room. She stood in front of Gina, put both arms under her armpits and lifted.

'Pull her chair out and shove the wheelchair in.'

Anna pushed Gina's chair to one side and rushed forward with the wheelchair; Maria eased Gina back into it and stopped to catch her breath.

'Go, make that tea, make it as strong as you can and

come after me. Make about half a pint.'

Maria turned the wheelchair so that she could pull it backwards and hauled it down the aisle for about thirty yards. It was hard going across the grass but with the chair tipped back a little she made good progress.

Taking a breather, Maria leaned down towards Gina who was still rigid in the chair.

'I'm taking you away from it. Hang on, keep fighting. It should get better soon.'

Maria grabbed the handles again and hauled the chair another stretch, taking them to the edge of the fair, out of the crowd and at least sixty yards from the track of the ley line. She could see Anna making her way through the crowd clutching a flask.

She stopped and waited. Moving back in front of Gina, she took her pulse again and listened to her breathing. Maybe it was a little less laboured and her pulse had slowed a little.

When Anna arrived, she poured a small amount of the tea into the cup and took it to Gina's lips. Nothing happened, her lips didn't move.

'We'll have to go further,' said Maria. 'You push and I'll pull.'

They heaved the chair another fifty yards and stopped again for breath. Maria dipped her finger in the tea and dabbed some liquid on Gina's lips. This time there was a slight movement. Maria felt the pulse again.

'It's slowing a bit. If I tip the chair back slightly see if you can get her to drink.'

'What's so special about camomile tea?'

'It has something in it that blocks adrenaline. She's scared, frightened out of her mind. The body reacts by making adrenaline; that's why her pulse is so fast. The tea will block the effect a bit. I can't think of anything else that might work. If she was in hospital there are drugs we could give her, but the hospital's miles away.'

Slowly Gina's colour changed and her breathing

became easier. As the liquid touched her lips she drank a little. In a few minutes she had swallowed half a cup.

'How fast does it work?'

Maria took her pulse again.

'It's down to a hundred and twenty,' she said. 'I've no idea how fast it works. The trouble is that adrenaline does other things. It makes your heart go faster but it also sends more blood to your muscles and diverts it away from your gut, so even if we get the tea in she may not absorb it very quickly. I can't think of anything else we can do.'

Mother and daughter watched for another minute, trying to detect any change in Gina.

'Why did you move her down here?'

'It's too complicated to explain right now, love. There's something evil in this field and it's down the other end.'

'I didn't think you believed in that sort of stuff.'

Maria laughed.

'I didn't, but this is different. Did you get what you wanted?'

Anna looked downcast.

'No, not at all. We'd barely started and suddenly she went rigid and I didn't know what to do. Then you came.'

Gina gasped, spluttered for a moment and then took another deep breath.

'Are you beginning to feel better?' said Maria. 'It would be good if you could drink some more of the tea, it helps get rid of the adrenaline.'

A half strangled 'thank you' came from Gina but over the next twenty minutes as more tea was drunk and the adrenaline was dissolved by her own body processes she was able to manage a few more words.

It was almost an hour later before she was able to ask, 'How did you know what to do?'

'I'm a nurse. I've worked in a cardiac ward and I had

a good idea what was wrong.' By then Sam had arrived and he and Anna had found some folding chairs so that the three of them could sit around the wheelchair. Slowly the story came out and the significance of the ley line became clear, which explained why Maria had dragged the chair-bound Gina to the edge of the fair.

'Everything I've read says the lines are only a few yards wide, six or seven in most cases. Maria guessed that the spirit can only function close to the line. Don't ask me why but it seems to have been a good guess. Your tent is not right on the line but it's close. I think you must be more sensitive than most and you have blue eyes, which seems to be important.'

'Blue eyes?'

'Everyone we've come across that has been affected has had blue eyes.'

'Were they as bad as me?'

'It's hard to say.'

'Why?'

'Most of them are dead; the only ones we think are alive are a group of schoolboys. They broke the school record for cross-country. They were running away from it.'

Gina laughed; laughed so much she almost fell off the chair.

'Feel a bit better now, do we?'

'I'm glad to know that someone lived. Seriously, this thing, whatever it is, frightens the hell out of people and they die? Is that what happens?'

Sam looked at Maria but her glance was quite clear; it said 'you tell her'.

'Each case I know about has caused someone to run, or panic and take some avoiding action, often with some tragic consequence. Is there any chance you can explain what happened to you?'

Gina turned to Maria.

'How long does that tea work?'

'It blocks adrenaline a bit, but it is destroyed in the body quite quickly so whatever you had on board will mostly have gone by now. I imagine you'll be OK, as long as you don't get another dose.'

'Easier said than done. My motorhome is very close to where you said the line runs and my pitch is not much better.'

'It's moving away.'

'How fast? Have I got to picnic out here for the rest of the week?'

Sam scratched his head.

'As far as I can tell it moves about half a mile a day, roughly.'

'So it might not be safe by tonight? Could I persuade one of you to pull my caravan down this end?'

'No problem,' said Sam. 'I don't know how you feel about this but is there any way you can describe what happened? Maria and Anna saw it from the outside but what was going on in your head?'

For a second Gina's face was vacant and then slowly she focused.

'It sounds stupid to say but it's hard to describe. I couldn't see anything. One moment I was looking at Anna and the next thing, it was as though something big and black had come out of nowhere right at me. There wasn't time to dodge it. I think I squeezed Anna's hand, gripping on tight in case I was hit backwards.'

'Very tight,' said Anna. 'I thought you were going to crush my fingers. That's when I thought something had gone wrong.'

'It enveloped me like a cloud, as though I was in a pitch black room.'

'Any sort of shape? Anything you would recognise again?'

'It was nothing, just a massive blackness, but it covered me completely. I couldn't see anything.'

She stopped for a moment, put her hand to her head and shook her head slightly.

'Everything after that was visceral, an awful feeling in my stomach. I could feel my heart fluttering; I could hardly breath. It was a, I don't know what, a terrible, terrifying fear, completely overwhelming. I couldn't think, I couldn't move. Everything stopped. If I had been able to I guess I'd have worried I was having a stroke or something but I couldn't think at all. I was frightened out of my mind. The only sensible thought I had was that I wasn't dead because I could hear myself breathing. That was all I could hear.'

'When did the blackout start to lift?'

'The next thing I knew I was being pulled along in the chair outside. I couldn't feel anything or think. How long did it go on for? I haven't any idea.'

Sam looked across to Anna.

'It must have been at least ten minutes. It took me two minutes to take her pulse and I did it twice because I didn't believe it at first, and that was after I'd got my hands out of her grip. After that, Mum arrived and she examined Gina and I went to get the chair. Then we got her into it and pulled her along here. Actually, it was probably more like fifteen minutes or maybe even longer.'

Gina looked at Anna.

'Why didn't it get you?'

'Brown eyes,' said Maria. 'She has brown eyes.'

'OK,' said Sam, 'here's the plan. I'll move the caravan if you'll tell me where the car keys are and then at least you'll have somewhere to rest.'

'You'll do no such thing,' said Maria.

'Why not?'

'Blue eyes, idiot. You stay here and I'll move the van. There is one good thing; there don't seem to have been any more panics. Everything over there seems to be running normally. Do you think it runs out of steam?'

Gina pulled the keys out of her pocket.

'You'll need these.' She turned to Sam. 'You've obviously been chasing this thing for a while. What happens next?'

Sam watched Maria walk back through the fair.

'I don't really know. I just know which way it's heading. All I had in mind was to see what might be in the way, assess the risk and see if it could be reduced in some way. So far I haven't had much luck but at least we've found Anna and no-one's been hurt.'

'When I've got my breath back can I help?'

'The more the merrier. At least you believe it exists, which is more than I can say for my colleagues or my boss.'

CHAPTER 26

Where next?

Sam left Anna and Maria with Gina; Anna had some explaining to do and Maria wanted to make sure that Gina had fully recovered. Despite several attempts none of them could persuade Gina to see a doctor, either locally or at a hospital, so Maria stayed with her until evening.

When he got home, Sam phoned HQ and after some negotiation persuaded them that he did need a week's holiday. The various inquests were unlikely to happen until after Christmas and Sam had put in too many extra hours recently. By evening, he had it arranged.

His next move was to start some much more detailed work on the path of the line. Using maps on the Web and all the other information he could gather, he tried to work out where the next big risk might be. As he worked, he kept coming back to the key question - how do you stop the thing, how do you get rid of it? The chances of persuading anyone else to believe in the threat seemed remote, even with Gina's testimony. He had to do it alone, he was sure of that. If he was with someone else and he froze then they might well get the full force of the thing. He couldn't take that risk.

Less than ten miles from the fairground was the boys boarding school and nearer than that were the playing fields. A rugby match being played with that thing in the middle of it was a horrific prospect. The cross-country course was an anomaly, he discovered. Local agricultural work had put the normal course out of use and the race had been temporarily moved to an area that made the boys run across the line. Sheer chance had brought four blue-eyed boys onto the ley line at exactly the wrong moment.

Sam spent the evening going over everything he knew, or might have guessed, about ley lines and the thing he was chasing. He phoned Maria twice, to make sure that Gina was OK and to hear if she had any further inspiration as to what they were up against.

After the second call his phone rang again. Once more it was Maria, but from outside Gina's motorhome this time.

'I don't think she's going to be any more help, Sam. We've been over it several times. What is interesting is that this experience was nothing like she'd had before. I don't know whether any of this medium, fortune telling stuff is real but whatever she was feeling when she was doing that stuff is nothing remotely like this.'

'I thought it might turn out like that but it was worth a shot, I guess.'

'You want to know something else?'

'Go on.'

'I bet you don't find that black car—the one Sanders thought he was swerving to miss. I think it was the same black thing that came over Gina. The difference is that the Sanders's were moving and by the time they'd swerved, they'd missed it. If the line really is a few yards wide that swerve was probably enough. After seeing what it did to Gina I don't blame them swerving.'

'It was still bloody awful driving.'

'Yes, maybe but another thought crossed my mind and I'm glad I thought of it rather than you having to tell me.'

Where is she going now? thought Sam.

'What?'

'Well, it's possible that the thing got to John as well.

He might have been standing there frozen. If Gina is anything to go by he would have been dead anyway.'

'I didn't realise that he had blue eyes.'

'Quite a charming blue.'

'Wouldn't he have run?'

'Not sure. I suppose no-one could be sure what they'd do but John didn't tend to run, he usually tried to stand up to things. There's another thing too, the dog. If the dog tried to run John would have held her back. She's still quite young, he was very anxious to train her to behave on roads. He'd have dug his heels in and pulled the lead back, he wouldn't have let the dog run loose.'

'Whatever you do don't tell Anna. She might never forgive herself.'

There was a long silence at the end of the phone.

'Are you OK?' he said.

'Yes, I was just thinking. Thanks for that Sam. If you don't mind, if she asks, tell her the line goes down the far side of the road. It may not cross her mind but she is quite bright and after seeing Gina, she's bound to think about it.'

'She probably won't ask me but if she does, I'll stick to your version.'

Sam put the phone down and looked at his map again. After the fairground, the line crossed a couple of fields and then a road. After a few more fields, it passed down a long shallow valley and then ran past the side of a small village, across the playing fields and on to the school grounds. It ran within a hundred yards of the school.

At least it's not running through a dormitory or a classroom, thought Sam.

What to do, that was the crucial question. He toyed with the idea of talking to Joyce. Whatever it was that her husband had done in the past, both of them thought that it stopped spirits in their tracks. The problem with that approach was that Joyce would want to be in on any attempt to stop the thing, and Joyce had blue eyes. There was no way he could take that risk. There was also the small fact that her husband had been an ordained priest. Did that give him special powers or some sort of immunity? One thing for sure, you could bet that wouldn't extend to police officers.

He glanced at his notes from the night before. I'd freeze, that's for sure, he thought. Medal or no medal, the moment in front of that gun still stuck with him, still haunted him. He had spent his life since then avoiding situations where someone else might have to rely on him in a crisis.

He tried to imagine meeting this thing; wished he had a name for it, a label, something that could be written down. A picture would have been good, something he could stick on the wall, like public enemy number one. All the witnesses who were still alive had described something happening very fast. Being in a car or on the motorbike didn't sound like a good idea. It wasn't going to help the world very much if he reacted like Mr Sanders and hit a tree. Even if he froze and didn't swerve, there was a fair chance he'd end up crashing. If he froze on his feet, what then? He'd be stuck with the thing for a while. Think, he said to himself, if it moves half a mile a day then that's about 30 yards in an hour, so a yard every two minutes. The ley line is only a few yards wide but the thing affected Gina and she was at least thirty yards away from the line. Let's imagine that you can feel it from thirty yards away, so that's thirty to get to you and another thirty to get past and away behind you. Sixty yards is two hours and it might be worse than that. What if running into the thing slowed it down?

If Sam held it in one place for a while would it give up? Would it pull the thing out of the ground so that it could fade away? How long could a person survive if they were in the grip of the thing? Some of the old people on the coach were killed in a few minutes but they were old people and they had bad hearts to start with.

What was the thing? It came from the slaughtered herd—collected fear jammed into a small space. Was it trapped by the ley line or was that a conduit, a pipe the thing could travel down, a line of least resistance? It held the thing in some way because it didn't spread sideways, only along the line. If it could be pulled out of the line then maybe it would dissipate, like a herd spreading out as they run, opening into a wider space and losing their fear. Images filled his head of cattle running, crowded together, forced by each swept alomg in the charge by the others until they gradually spread out, making enough space to lose their collective fear.

The more he thought about it the more convinced he became that if he froze the thing would not be able to move on and somehow it would be stopped. Everyone else had either died or run. What if it killed him? What if he died like the passengers on the coach? They couldn't run, they were trapped on the coach. One had tried to run but couldn't move fast enough. The old lady who died in the toilet was trapped in the building. They had wanted to run but they died very quickly. Just standing still was not enough, he had to stay alive long enough for the fear to dissipate. He remembered the dead rabbits by the burial mound. Four rabbits in a cluster; surely they were not killed by a fox or any other predator because they hadn't been eaten. They must have been hit by the thing and scared to death on the spot. Would that happen to him?

Freezing was only part of the solution; he had to find some way to resist so he could stay alive long enough for the thing to evaporate. He called Maria again.

'All that stuff you were saying to Gina about adrenaline and camomile tea, what does the tea do?'

'It was the best I could come up with in a hurry. Adrenaline raises blood pressure, heart rate and cardiac output; beta-blockers are drugs that block that. Camomile does some of the same things.'

'So if you'd had a pocket full of beta blockers that would have been better.'

'If I'd had an intravenous one and a syringe handy, yes, maybe. Pills wouldn't work fast enough, especially because the adrenaline shunts the blood out of the gut to shove it round the muscles. If I'd given her pills she wouldn't have absorbed them fast enough to do any good. Where are you going with this?'

'Nowhere, I'm trying to get my head around it.'

He put the phone down and the beginnings of a plan formed in his mind. How could he get hold of some beta-blocker tablets and how many of the things should he take? There was no way he was likely to persuade a doctor and if he went to a hospital he had no idea how to fake whatever symptoms would do the trick. He searched the internet for a while and was not much the wiser. He'd almost given up on the idea when he remembered a friend who played the violin who said he took some when he had stage fright before a big concert.

A bit of hunting around found his friend's phone number and a rather odd conversation followed.

'It does calm you, I definitely tremor less. What do you need it for? Are you learning to shoot? It's not allowed in shooting competitions.'

'It sounds daft,' said Sam, thinking fast. 'I'm doing some work with maps, trying to plot some very detailed stuff. I keep finding my hands shake too much. I know it sounds half baked and I'm sure there's some other way of doing it, I figured this might be quickest.'

'You're lucky I've still got some. Get your skates on

and get over here and I'll let you have a couple of tablets, see if it does the trick.'

Sam dashed out and twenty minutes later had two Atenolol tablets wrapped in silver foil.

He spent another half an hour on the internet looking at overdose of beta-blockers and concluded that two tablets wouldn't kill him. Might not save me either, he thought, but every little helps. So long as I still freeze when it hits me, it might stop it. How long would he need to stand there and would the beta-blockers stop him freezing? Impossible to tell, but the pills are supposed to work for twenty-four hours. That might be long enough, which means, he thought, it would have to be done at night. Anyone standing in one place in the daytime might seem odd. It has to be at night and somewhere out of the way. Standing frozen in front of someone's window for a few hours would get him arrested, or some poor soul would come to see what was wrong with him and be frightened to death. That wouldn't do at all.

He looked at the map again trying to reconcile the geography with the timeline. It had to be done before it got anywhere near the village or the school. He found his finger settling on the long shallow valley, a little way up the line from the village and the boarding school.

CHAPTER 27

The Valley

Looking at the valley from the road, the lower end showed a long steadily rising grass field, fringed with trees on either side. The incline was very gradual and only rose a few hundred feet before it disappeared into the trees on the slight ridge less than a mile away. Sam parked the motorbike and walked up to the ridge. From the road, it looked like a steady incline all the way up but once he was on foot he could see the gentle undulations. About half way to the top there was a small dip. As he walked forwards, with an occasional glance back, he could see that for a short distance the road became invisible. After another fifty yards rising further up the field, a backward glance picked up the road again. From there onwards it was a steady climb to the top. The ridge was covered with a mass of trees and scrub. Sam spent a few minutes struggling with brambles and other impediments and gave up. The thought of trying to take on some invisible entity at night amongst these hazards would be too much. He eased his way back to the grass, trying to avoid being tangled or stabbed by the unruly vegetation.

When he got back to the small dip halfway down he decided this was the ideal spot, out of sight of the road and unlikely to attract attention. A careful study of his map made certain of the exact position of the line. The only problem might be the weather. If it rained hard, did the valley become a small river and did this dip fill with water? That would have to wait until he had a detailed weather forecast for the night he would try to take on the terror. The only other issue was timing. So long as it passed through here in the night, he mentally re-ran the calculations in his head, but he still didn't feel completely confident. He made sure he had the map reference recorded exactly and set off home to re-do calculations with the computer.

The valley was a little over half a mile long. The sprit moved about half a mile a day so there had to be a good chance of catching it. He reworked all his calculations and plotted his best estimate for the arrival of the thing in the valley. Even with a margin for error it looked like he would catch it at night. OK, that was good, no one would see, but it was also scary, because no one would see. Everything ran around in his head; if someone saw him they might stop him, but if he was alone he might die. If he were dying and someone found him then they might die too. Well, he thought grimacing, if I do die, at least it won't be my problem.

If you die then who will stop it? The question formed in his head and refused to go away until it occurred to him to write it all down. It took an hour of typing and retyping before he was happy. If I die and they find this, at least they'll believe me, he thought. Maybe they could move everyone out of the way until it gets to the sea. There might be some very surprised fishes but no one has said there are ley lines in the sea.

Should he bring a tent? Would it work inside a tent? It seemed to have penetrated the Sanders's car and Gina's tent, so a tent wouldn't keep it out. He might fall asleep, would that matter? He didn't want to wake up wondering if he'd dreamt the whole thing, being too comfortable sounded like a bad idea, even if he did have to wait a while.

Would it make more sense to walk towards the thing, not worry about being in the dip or anywhere else for that matter? Get there on the day it was likely to arrive, walk up the valley slowly and wait for it to hit.

That had to be the best plan.

When the day arrived the weather forecast was not the least bit encouraging. He watched the man on the TV twice and looked at several forecasts on the internet. They all said the same thing, a good chance of snow.

Only one thing for it, wear the right gear. He worked through his wardrobe selecting warm underwear, then the trousers he'd used years ago for traffic duty. On top he had a vest and then a shirt left over from learning to ski, supposedly with great wicking properties, and then a sweater and his thick waterproof jacket. He did think about the High Visibility traffic jacket, designed to keep anything out, but it would also be visible from miles away and he didn't need visibility. His best guess was that the thing would be in the valley some time after six in the evening, which was ideal, apart from the snow.

He swallowed the two Atenolol tablets, taking them while he was still at home so as to give them plenty of time to absorb and before any adrenaline got into his system. He packed a small backpack with two Thermos flasks, one with normal tea and the other with the camomile stuff that Maria had talked about. He put plenty of sugar in both. He filled his pockets with chocolate bars, four in each side pocket. With cold fingers he might fumble and drop one in the dark, so best to have plenty. He picked a thick cap with earmuffs and, as an afterthought, his old ski goggles. He wrapped a scarf round his face. Then he thought about driving and removed the scarf and jacket for the journey. He did think about the motorbike but settled for the car. He could park at the bottom of the valley and if anything happened, the car would be found and he could leave a note.

As he drove away from home the sky had taken on a livid leaden look; the cloud base getting lower and the wind freshening. The first flakes of snow whipped across his windscreen a mile later. After that, with every yard he went, the snow came harder. The road was dry, so at first the flakes skittered across it, catching here and there in potholes, but mostly pitching on the verge and in the hedges, making the sides of the road pale in his headlights.

He felt relaxed. Maybe it was the effect of the pills. He wished he'd had enough spare to try them for a day beforehand, just to know what to expect. Maybe it wasn't the pills, perhaps it was the commitment to action. This thing had been on his mind every hour of the last few weeks but tonight, one way or another, it had to end. In the back of his mind was the nagging fear that it might be the end of him; did that make it more likely the thing would get him? There was only one way to find out. The pills were supposed to disconnect the anxiety from your body. They give them to people when they have heart attacks so that their anxiety doesn't make things worse. That's why he'd taken them. Fragments of things he'd read kept popping into his mind, but soon he had to settle down to driving carefully as the snow came down harder. There was no point in crashing before even getting there.

There was a rough layby a hundred yards from the foot of the valley. He parked carefully in the middle of the space, not feeling the need to be neat and tidy at this time of night. Considering the possibility of heavier snow, he also wanted the car to be visible and not get written off by some snowplough early in the morning.

He texted the map location to Maria. She was working nights this week. If she saw it she might wonder why he was sending it at this time of night. No matter, he had promised.

When he switched off the ignition and the wipers stopped, snow began to accumulate on the front window. He watched it for a moment, marvelling at the way that individual flakes, each with their own unique pattern, rapidly became part of something so even and smooth. He shoved the driver's seat as far back as he could make it go. That gave him enough room to change his shoes for heavy boots and struggle into his big coat while he was still inside the car. He wrapped the scarf around his neck, tucking it in to block any little gaps. He then rammed the cap on his head, folded down the earflaps and picked up the rucksack and gloves from the passenger seat. He found the card that he had already written his mobile number and police identification on, as well as a brief note as to where he was going. With a final flourish, he carefully placed it on the front dash.

'Not that anyone will see that through the snow,' he muttered as he opened the door.

Once outside he locked the car, swung the backpack on to his shoulders, pulled on his gloves and set off along the road. In a few minutes he was through the gate and into the valley. Taking his bearings from the trees on either side, he turned up the hill, knowing that he was right on the ley line.

When he was facing uphill the snow came at an angle from ahead and to the right, whipping across his face, stinging and making it hard to see. He turned his back to the weather for a moment and dug his goggles out of a pocket, put them on, took them off and adjusted the strap to suit the thicker cap before putting them back on and turning to face the snow again. He eased one turn of his scarf up over his face so that the only skin left visible was a tiny space over his cheekbone. I should have grown a beard, he thought.

By now the snow was an inch deep but easy to walk through. Ahead of him he could see very little and he used his torch occasionally to check that he was on track.

'How the hell will I even know if that black thing comes over me?' he muttered to himself.

How far up should he go? That was the question. The thing wasn't due for a couple of hours at least. It had seemed simple when he walked up the valley in daylight and sunshine. Walk up the hill, wait for the thing to arrive. How hard could it be?

In the dark, in heavy snow, it seemed to be a very different proposition; if it weren't so dark it would be a white out. What do you call a white out in the dark? I should have brought something to sit on and the tent would have been a good idea. He crested the small ridge half way up and walked a few yards into the little dip. The snow was much thicker underfoot, the undulation in the ground providing enough shelter to take some of the momentum off the wind and allow the flakes to settle.

It's no different from traffic duty, he thought. Well, except doing that you get to wave your arms around. What's to stop you waving your arms around now? At least my mind is still working, he thought. OK, before you start doing calisthenics, check how things are. Feet? Warm, no problem. Face? Feels fine. Hands? Feel OK. So far so good. A little walk up the ridge, he thought. He moved forwards twenty yards and found himself back in the full force of the wind. He started to step backwards down the slope and then thought, I can turn my back. If this thing arrives, which way I'm facing isn't going to matter. Standing back to the wind might be a good idea; I'm less likely to freeze to death before it gets here. He turned down the slope and his face felt a degree or two warmer, as though someone had turned a fan heater on about a mile away.

With his back to the wind his thoughts became a little clearer and he unpacked the backpack, flattened it out and sat on it to drink the tea. How much of the camomile was the right amount? There was no way of doing more research now. He filled the thermos cup up and then poured another half a cup of ordinary tea into the cup from the second flask. Drinking the camomile first he almost spat it out. It had an odd flavour, like grass or some vegetation. He grimaced and drank it as though it were medicine. It is medicine, he said to himself, get on with it. He followed that with the more familiar tea, made to the standard builder's recipe—hot, strong and sweet. Sitting on the ground, he found that most of the wind went over his head. He pulled one of his gloves and sleeves apart for a moment to look at his watch and was surprised to find that more than an hour had elapsed since he left the car. Thinking that the camomile might make him sleepy, he found the energy to stand up and saw that a drift of snow six inches high had piled up against his back. If it keeps on like this I can make an igloo, he thought.

He faced into the storm again and walked up to the peak of the ridge. It was impossible to see anything beyond his torchlight. He stood for a moment, straining his eyes into the driving snow and then retreated, turning his back and retracing his steps. Walking over the same ground twice made it feel a bit like sentry duty, but it passed the time. When he had had enough of pacing he went back to sitting down.

Two hours after midnight he had been sitting for half an hour. He'd drunk almost all the camomile tea and eaten one bar of chocolate. He had tried singing for a while, to make sure he was still awake. At his back there was now a pile of snow almost two feet high and it was beginning to wrap around him like a blanket. Out of the full force of the wind, and sheltered by this drift, he had begun to understand how Inuit survived blizzards. Five minutes later he had begun to think he was getting too comfortable, so stood up, meaning to stretch his muscles a little to help him stay awake.

Easing the stiffness in his muscles for a moment

made him think. What did he imagine would happen? The thing would hit him and then what? I'll freeze. Yes said the rest of his mind, then what? The thing will be stuck. It will have to stay put with me and that will drag it out of the ground. Then what? For a moment his resolve faltered. Then it will dissipate. It needs to be in the ground to stay alive; if it is dragged out into the air it will lose concentration, dissipate, like a stampede coming to the end of its energy. Doubts crept into his head. Why would it do that? How did he know?

As he struggled to hush his doubts, it hit him. He had the torch off at the time, saving the battery, but he was surprised by the sense of blackness. It was a different kind of darkness. The night filled with snowflakes was just as black but somehow *it* was tangible. This other darkness was a void, not so much blackness, as an absence of everything. Nothing Sam had ever experienced was anything like this. He had about five seconds in which to appreciate the feeling before the anxiety struck. Those seconds were long enough to think that he'd fallen off the planet into outer space; something he'd imagined several times as a child, when he had wanted to be an astronaut.

The rising fear was, as Gina had said, something visceral. Unlike Gina he could still think, just. A small voice in his head observed that the pills and the camomile must have been doing something.

He tried to break it down, pull it apart and work out what was there, besides the awful fear. He expected to see visions of frightened animals running, falling, being maimed and slaughtered, but there were no visions, just a void. There was no sound either. The gale seemed to have disappeared and he stopped feeling the cold. He couldn't feel anything. He couldn't even think how to move his arms and legs. If he concentrated very hard, he could detect that he was still breathing. If it was like this after taking the pills, what kind of hell must it be for those caught unawares?

Thinking very slowly, desperately trying to keep a sense of self and not let his whole being fall into this empty space that seemed to surround him, he managed to convince himself that he had frozen and not run. There was absolutely no sense of movement. He made another enormous effort to move his legs but nothing happened.

It's you and me, he managed to think, and neither of us is going anywhere.

He had no sense of the passage of time but he did feel himself getting tired. Was it the tea kicking in? All the material he'd read on the internet said it was a sedative, or was he just getting weary? Not having any sense of time and thinking so slowly made it impossible to understand what was happening to him. Did he stop feeling the cold before his face felt hot? Was it sweat running down the back of his neck or was it snow getting in?

To anyone watching, if they had been close enough to see through the snow and armed with enough light to penetrate the dark, all they would have seen was a tall figure with his back gradually being covered with snow. If they had returned many hours later, they would have seen the figure bend at the knees and drop into a kneeling position. Sam was completely unaware of that movement. By then he was in the void, almost unable to think but becoming aware of heat rather than cold. By the time he had sunk back on his haunches so much snow had piled up against him that he could not have fallen backwards if he had tried. He was locked in an icy cocoon.

It was about that time that Maria stopped for her break and happened to look at her phone. She stared at the text message for some time. What did it mean? Surely Sam wasn't out tracing the line on a night like this? She tried texting him back but didn't really expect an answer because she thought he was probably in bed.

There was nothing she could do, her shift didn't end for another couple of hours and then she had to get home through the snow. What time do they start the snowploughs, she wondered?

The storm raged around Sam. At his back the snow was now a solid mound starting at his shoulders and angling down to the ground behind him. On his left side the drift curled elegantly around him, sculpted into fascinating shapes by the wind. If it had been symmetrical, he might have been mistaken for an angel with wings folded around his face. Inside the snowdrift the cold was doing its best to extract every ounce of heat from Sam's back and freeze him into a state of hypothermia from which he would never wake.

The fear gripped his mind, from where Sam was struggling to keep in the game. His thought processes were so slow that he had no notion of time and no sensation of his body, but he was still there. Conflict raged in his organs. The fear holding on to almost all of his nervous system was doing its best to flood his body with adrenalin, hydrocortisone and thyroxin. If Sam had been in a normal state his heart and muscles would have long ago succumbed to the onslaught of these hormones. Sam, however, had taken beta-blockers and that disconnected some of the impact. He should have had a raging fever by now but as fast as the fear heated his blood, the snow on his back cooled it, so that an uneasy equilibrium was established. Sam was alive but he was barely aware of it, caught in the middle of a battle between the awful fear on the inside and the snowstorm outside.

By the time the snowploughs were out the battle for Sam's body and soul still hung in the balance, with equal points going to the fear and the snow. Sam, as far as he had any awareness, was a passenger in a body that was possessed by other forces. The one thing that bode well was that he was still at least partly vertical. His tendency to freeze with fear had done enough to keep his torso upright, so only one side of him was covered in snow. If he had lain flat he would have been covered and might have suffocated even if he hadn't frozen.

When Maria left the hospital it had stopped snowing and the plough and the traffic had cleared enough roads to make driving home possible. When she got near she remembered Sam's text and took the risk of driving through the deeper snow to go past the police station and his house, but she could see no sign of his car at either. Immediately she got home she rang his landline and both mobiles. She got the answering machine at the station and on his official mobile. She rang the main police station too but all they could say was that Sam was on holiday. She told them that she'd had a text message in the night but they thought it was probably a glitch with the phone reception.

'That's the thing with text messages,' the operator said, treating Maria as if she were an idiot, 'they're often delayed. You don't even know exactly when they might get through.'

Maria woke Anna. It took a few minutes to get her to pay attention but eventually she got across that Sam might have gone out to try to intercept the spirit. She made Anna follow her steps as she plotted the reference he had sent on the map and then calculated when the thing might get there. After doing everything twice neither of them were in any doubt that Sam and the thing had probably met in the night.

After the conversations she had already had with the police it seemed very unlikely that they would be able to get anyone interested in finding him.

They loaded some extra blankets in the car. Just as they were about to set off Anna stopped Maria.

'Mum, that map point is in the middle of a field. If

he's bad how will we move him?'

'I don't know, sort of drag him or something.'

'What about my old sledge, you know, the red plastic one? I know where it is.'

She dashed back into the garage and was back a minute later with the sledge, which she threw in the back of the car.

'If this turns out to be a wild goose chase, we can always go tobogganing!'

The road to the valley was slippery but open and luckily there was no traffic. When they got to the lay by there was a car under the snow. They pulled off the road and Anna scraped the snow off the rear number plate. It was Sam's car and there was no one in it.

'That settles it, he must be in the field,' said Maria. 'You pull the sledge and I'll grab the blankets.'

She pushed and tried to open the gate but it proved easier to climb over it.

'We'll have to get it open if he's in a bad way.'

'I know, Mum, but let's find him first.'

From the lower slope they could see no sign of anyone; a smooth sheet of snow stretched away from them up the hill.

'The line went right up the middle didn't it, Mum?'

'Almost exactly, so let's start in the middle and go straight up. Let's hope he's not buried under this or we might not see him.'

They set off through the snow. Fortunately it was crisp and fluffy enough that they could make their way through it without too much effort.

After about a hundred yards they saw the top of Sam's cap.

To say they ran through the snow would be an overstatement but they did cover the next bit a good deal faster than any other stretch. They were confronted by a solid mass of snow, with Sam in the middle. Maria scraped what she could off his face, removed the goggles and tried to see into his eyes. Trying to test pupil reactions in the middle of a snowfield is not easy, especially when you have to open the patient's eyelids yourself. Knowing the patient and wanting desperately to see their pupils react to light made the task more complicated. In that second Maria realised that she desperately wanted Sam to be alive. Three times she tried the test, covering his eye for a few seconds with her hand then rapidly allowing light onto his face while she held his eyelid open. Eventually she convinced herself that the pupil really did react.

'Phone 999, call an ambulance. If they can get to the bottom of the field we can see if we can bring him down while they're on the way.'

While Anna phoned, Maria attempted to expose enough of Sam's wrist to be able to take his pulse. Her own fingers were freezing by the time she decided that his heart rate was somewhere over 120, not as high as Gina's had been, but Sam had been here all night. At least he was alive.

When Anna got off the phone they both pushed him on to his side, quite a struggle with the snow mound around him but they got his legs out from under him and straightened them out.

'I wish I had some idea what I was doing,' said Maria. 'I don't know if he has hypothermia or if he's still under the spell of that thing.'

'Should we try to move him sideways, to get away from the ley line?'

'If we can move him at all.'

'If we can go straight down and sort of sideways a bit, by the time we get to the gate we'll be at least fifty yards beyond the line.'

In a flurry of snow, falling over, rolling, pulling and every other movement they could think of, they eventually had most of Sam's body on the sledge. Maria wrapped one of the blankets around him and they set off, with Anna pulling and Maria pushing until the sledge crested the little ridge and it started to go downhill under its own momentum. Steering was hardly exact but they did crab across the hill enough to make the gate without Sam falling off, or either of them being hurt. It took five minutes to clear the snow from the gate and get it open enough to struggle through and wait for the ambulance.

Five minutes later Maria was following the blue light back to the hospital that she'd left only a few hours ago and ten minutes after that she was sending Anna to find some coffee. Maria's night shift was starting to catch up with her and it was hard enough to try to explain what had happened to Sam, without wanting to fall asleep as well.

CHAPTER 28

Recovery

Maria told the paramedics that they had found Sam by the side of the road; no sense in letting things get complicated at this stage. In the hospital she followed Sam to intensive care and watched as monitors were attached and the doctors started to assess his condition. Fortunately, because she knew all the people involved, she was able to bypass all the usual questions about her relationship to the patient. She simply said he was the local policemen, she lived nearby and she had found him in the snow.

The doctor finished his examination and came to talk to Maria.

'Bit of a puzzle your bobby here. He's been out in the snow for a few hours from what you say and one might expect him to be hypothermic but actually, if anything, his temperature is on the high side. His blood sugar is down and his blood pressure and pulse are up a bit. I think my best guess is that he had some sort of fever that made him faint but it increased his metabolism and kept him hot, but it chewed up a lot of energy. He's exhausted but otherwise OK. We'll top up his fluids and get him stable, do some blood work and see what we can find. Do you know if he has any next of kin?'

Maria thought for a moment.

'I've had to talk to him a fair bit recently but he's never mentioned anyone. I'll call the police HQ later on and see what I can turn up. Right now, I'm going to go home to sleep. My daughter, Anna, will stay and call me if anything happens; I feel a bit responsible for him. I'll let you know if I find any relatives.'

That seemed to satisfy enough official curiosity and allowed Maria to leave. Later in the afternoon she discovered that the police had no record of Sam's family. When she came back to the hospital in the evening Sam was showing signs of waking. She sat with him for an hour before going on her shift. Just before she left, he opened his eyes for a moment and she briefly got his attention.

'I told them I found you by the roadside,' she said. 'They think you must have had a fever of some sort that made you collapse. I've got to go to work now, I'll see you in the morning.'

Sam blinked and she thought she caught a hint of a smile.

Next morning he was in better shape, moved out of the ITU and in a normal ward, breathing on his own and sitting up.

Maria was still in her uniform and he almost didn't recognise her.

'We are a bit better this morning, I see.'

'How did you find me?'

'You sent me the map reference. When I didn't see your car at home I guessed where you must be. What happened?'

'I got there before dark, then it snowed and about half way through the night the thing arrived. After that, I don't know much. There was a terrible blackness, even though it was already very dark, with no visibility because of the snow. Somehow it was darker than dark. Black is the absence of colour but what I experienced must be what you get if you take the black away as well. It was sheer terror, I can't think of anything else to call it. I thought I might see the animals it came from, or something like that, but this thing is beyond that. Sort of distilled fear; what you'd get if you took away what you were scared of and left the fear itself. Fear for no reason.'

'I don't understand how you survived, you were there for about twelve hours. If Gina was anything to go by it should have killed you, plus the cold—that could have killed you anyway.'

'I cheated a bit. I took a couple of beta-blockers, after what you said, and some camomile tea. It seemed like a good idea.'

'I'm not going to ask where you got the pills; I don't think they're standard police issue. Did you have any idea what you were doing?'

'No, not really. I read a lot and listened to you,' he grinned. 'But don't feel responsible,' he said, as an exasperated frown crept across her face. 'The doctor thinks I must have had a virus of some sort that tried to put my temperature up at the same time as the snow was taking it down, so the two evened out.'

'I'm very glad I came looking for you. That sort of lucky equilibrium wouldn't have gone on much longer.'

'I've lost a stone,' he said. 'Probably do me good in the long run.'

'Why did you try such a barmy stunt? What made you think it would work?'

'I don't even know if it did.'

'Nothing's happened in the village or at the school. The kids were all out playing in the snow; the odd snowball fight but no riots, no deaths. If it was still going strong it should have had a field day.'

Sam laid back on the pillows and a slow smile crept across his face.

'I think you burned it out,' she said. 'How did you manage to stay there?'

For a moment, he lay with his eyes closed.

'What's the secret?' she said.

'Can I tell you another day? I can hardly keep my eyes open.'

She looked at him for a moment and, almost as a reflex, took his pulse. By the time she'd counted it he was fast asleep.

She came back in the evening, arriving an hour before her shift in the hope that she'd catch him awake.

She was standing at the end of the bed reading his charts when he opened his eyes. She moved around to the side of the bed and sat down.

'Are you feeling any better?'

'A little. I still feel very weary.'

'Can you manage to stay awake long enough to tell me the secret?'

'Only if you swear to never tell a soul.' For a second he looked straight at her 'And you have to promise to believe me.'

'Why wouldn't I believe you?'

'Because no one else ever has.'

'But this only happened a day ago.'

'No, it goes back ten years really. When I got my medal, because of that idiot shooting at us, I froze. I couldn't move a muscle. They said I was brave but really, I was frozen to the spot. I've never been able to convince anyone.'

He paused, holding her gaze and looking so serious that she knew she had to believe him. She squeezed his hand for encouragement.

'Go on.'

'That freezing has haunted me ever since. I've always been convinced that if I were in some dangerous situation it would happen again. I didn't dare put myself in a position where anyone else might have to rely on me. Eventually I got this job as a village bobby; somewhere I could work on my own and not be a risk to anyone else. It was a nice life until this thing came along. I thought that if that thing hit me and it was frightening then I'd freeze and it would be stuck with me. Of course I hadn't figured on actually freezing temperaturewise. I didn't know it was going to snow when I worked out the plan. By the time I had a weather forecast it was too late. Another day and it would have been in the village and the school.'

'And you don't think you were brave?'

'I couldn't think what else to do. Do you know that poem by Piet Hein?'

'No, amaze me.'

'Well I can't remember it exactly but the gist is that you can only be brave when you're scared, so not really brave at all. He puts it better than that.' He grinned.

'Hein was a physicist, a mathematical type but he wrote a couple of books full of short little poems he called Grooks. I should have learned it off pat so I could recite it to you. I wasn't brave I just did what I thought I could do that other people would find hard.'

'Like not running a mile in the same situation. I'm not sure I can cope with philosophy at this time of the day. My shift starts in half an hour; it's my last night on duty. I'll come and see you in the morning before I go home.'

'You do believe me don't you?'

'I promised I would but I'll have to think about it. I think the medical staff will want to keep you in bed for a day or two, even if your bloods are not full of little black holes or anything.'

She grinned at him.

'I'll tell the ward staff that if they have any trouble, all they have to do is yell at you and you'll freeze and stay in bed.' That dragged a weak smile from him.

It was two more days before a thinner and still weary Sam was picked up and taken home by Maria, and another day after that before he was well enough to collect his car.

CHAPTER 29

Ending

Sam cooked. It gave him something to concentrate on and with a bit of luck it would help him get his strength back. This time, instead of carefully chosen, nouvelle cuisine-style portions designed to produce flavour without weight gain, he went for what he thought of as autumnal comfort food. A massive beef stew for the main course and apple pie to follow.

The thing about a good stew was that you could work at it for four or five hours. If you had the time, and nothing else happened, then you could taste it several times an hour, add a dash of this or that, wallow in the anticipation and enjoy the aroma wafting around the house. If you were called away, no problem, turn off the heat and pick up the process when you got back. Stew was not simply a comfort food, it was a forgiving food. It let the lazy or distracted chef off lightly but at the same time it rewarded the person who hovered over it and lovingly refined the flavour.

Sam was doing just that when Maria turned up.

'Don't tell me you can smell it from home.'

She laughed. 'You're keeping yourself busy I see.'

'Feeding myself up. Got to get my stamina back.'

Maria looked around the kitchen, saw a container of ground coffee and asked,

'Were you about to make coffee?'

Sam glanced at the coffee, seeming surprised and taken aback. He saw Maria's face, picked up the coffee and laughed.

'I was about to put some in the stew.'

'What?'

'It adds a bit of depth. Sometimes, if I haven't browned the beef enough, or maybe it depends on the beef, or if the flavour seems to lack a bit of depth, I bung in a bit of coffee.'

'Ground coffee, just like that?'

'Yeah. You don't notice the grounds by the end, they all absorb into the gravy, and it gives them plenty of time to soak into everything. Don't look so amazed. I could be adding toffee and you'd think it was mad but look at the ingredients in some of these gravy things—caramel and such like. If it works bung it in, that's what I say.'

'You're full of surprises.'

'I'll take that as a compliment. What can I do for you? Apart from not having coffee ready.'

'I've been keeping track of all the local papers. To be completely accurate, Anna and Gina have been collecting all the local news, parish magazines and anything else they can lay their hands on from everywhere further down your ley line.'

'And?'

'There haven't been any reports. Absolutely nothing.'

He stirred the stew and tasted it. She watched his face as he tried to concentrate on the flavour. He dipped another spoon and tasted again, still frowning slightly.

'I thought you'd be pleased,' she said.

'I suppose I am, it's just that I don't know what it proves. How do we know it isn't still there, moving along, waiting to pounce?'

'How did you know it was there before? Only because things happened and now they haven't.'

'I wish I felt as though I'd beaten it. I've sat around in hospital and then here, trying to remember what happened. I can recall it getting dark and the snow starting. I had a drink, some of that tea and I think I ate one chocolate bar; I had four bars in each pocket and most of them are still there. You found me in the morning, almost twelve hours later, and my brain is a blank.'

'Are you sure you want to remember?'

'You mean because it might be so awful?'

'Yes. Maybe not remembering is a survival mechanism. People often find it hard to remember pain. They'll tell you they had it but mostly the experience fades into the background.'

'How can I tell if it's gone?'

She picked up a spoon and tasted the stew.

'Thought I'd check,' she said, 'in case you were completely distracted. Actually it's good, I can't taste the coffee at all.'

'That's because I hadn't put it in yet, I was just trying to decide if it needed it.'

He turned off the stove.

'I can't cook and think.'

'I don't think that came out quite right,' she said, 'but I know what you mean. Let's go back a step, forget about the night in the snow. What was your plan, whatever you thought you were doing? Why did you think it would work?'

Sam put a lid on the stew and sat down, lost in thought for a moment.

'Now you ask, I'm not sure it was completely clear in my mind. I thought there must be something in the work that Joyce did with her husband. As far as I could tell they simply got the spirits out of their normal environment and somehow that made them disappear. It was as though there was something that was sustaining them where they were and moving it starved the thing of whatever it was and it vanished. Maybe the prayers sent it to a better place, who knows? That was one side of it and the other was me.

'I know that when I'm afraid, I freeze. At least I know that's what happened when that guy was waving a gun around. I was convinced I wouldn't run, so the thing would have to fight me and that would keep it out of the ground. I thought I might die and that might kill it, or I might be able to resist it and it would run out of whatever keeps it going. I thought if I took the beta blockers and the camomile, the thing would get stuck out of the ground for longer. I think I sort of hoped it would wear itself out or something.'

'So you had no thought that it might scare you, and pick up strength from that; with you rooted to the spot where it can feed off your fear? No thought of that then?'

Sam looked a little sheepish.

'No, it never entered my head. It all sounds a bit foolish now. I think I did fight it, I can't remember. I thought the pills were bound to help. If they disconnect the mental fear from the bodily reaction, I thought the thing might find that a problem.'

'So you thought you'd feed it Beta-Blockers and that would do the trick. The drug companies will be proud of you, one more thing they can say that it cures.'

'OK, so it was a daft idea and it nearly killed me, but did it work?'

'I've told you, there's been nothing since.'

'I'll have to go and explore another day, when I'm sure I'll be strong enough.'

'I don't think it's a good idea but if you insist then I'm coming with you.'

Sam shrugged and smiled.

'I don't suppose I could stop you? What about Anna, does she still want to talk to her dad?'

'That's one thing you have cured. She thinks her whole idea was crazy and she thinks she almost killed Gina. The good news is that the two of them are best mates now. I've been very impressed with Gina. She looked after Anna when she could have ripped her off and since then she's been very brave. She insisted on going looking for the thing with Anna, ready to drag her away if they got a whiff of it.'

'That's crazy.'

'They deployed your secret weapon. Gina took Beta-Blockers, just in case. They've written it all down, where they've been, what they found.'

'I'm surprised you let Anna go off on a trip like that.'

'I couldn't have stopped her if I'd wanted to. I made her phone me every fifteen minutes. She's been very anxious to prove shat she's being responsible and grown up. They had more back up too. Gina persuaded one of the lads from the fair to drive them; a big lad with brown eyes, apparently.'

Sam stirred the stew for a moment and tasted it again.

'I'd still like to see for myself; drive down there and ask around a bit. I need to get it out of my system.'

'I'll drive you,' she said. 'It'll be easier than having to keep an eye on you and chasing after you.' Overnight, Sam read all the reports that Maria, Anna and Gina had gathered and the following day he set off with Maria and Anna to make further exploration of the ley line.

Most of the snow had gone, apart from a few pockets where it had drifted into shaded areas. They stopped briefly at the little valley and Sam walked back up the field to the place where he had stood. Maria and Anna soon saw him strolling back down, smiling, clutching his backpack and the two thermos flasks. They drove through the village and past the school before the road straightened out again and in another mile they were in a traffic jam.

As the car stopped, Maria could see Sam tense.

'Something must be up,' he said. 'There's no reason for traffic to be stopped here, it's just a little village.'

Occasional cars passed them in the other direction, appearing randomly, not in the kind of clusters that are created by traffic lights. They crept forwards, moving a few car lengths at a time, with Sam becoming more anxious as every minute passed. Finally they came to a barrier across the road and were diverted down a narrow street.

Sam was all for jumping out there and then but Maria dissuaded him. As they turned the next corner the car had to be stopped again. After three more short moves forward they discovered the problem—a big sign saying, "Car park for Market" with a very narrow turn in, that was causing all the cars to manoeuvre very carefully.

'We'd better park and explore,' said Sam. 'This is close to the timeline.'

The whole of the main street of the village was taken up with the market. What should have been a wide thoroughfare was full of market stalls and crowds.

After agreeing a time to meet back at the car, Sam and Maria left Anna to explore on her own. Many of the stalls featured work by local farmers and craftspeople, from pottery and woodcarving to glasswork and no end of cuddly toys. Some stalls played music, some had sound systems to amplify their sales pitches. They had flags and bunting to add to the general air of cheerful enthusiastic chaos. The one thing there was no sign of was any panic or aimless fear.

Sam tried to chat to as many stall holders as he could, asking how it was going, what was trade like, did they get any trouble? Everywhere he asked he got the same answer to that last question—no trouble, nice people, a good market to come to. Many of the stallholders were regulars.

Sam and Maria tried some of the food on sale, munching their way through pork rolls and pizzas before trying a crepe, made right in front of them, for dessert.

After two hours they had exhausted any interest in everything the market had to offer and set off back to the car. On the way they found Anna and the three of them detoured through the back streets of the village to find some peace from the crowds.

'Did you find anything?'

'Everything seems to have been very peaceful. It's great to see so many people having a good time.'

That wasn't enough for Anna.

'So is that it? It's all over, you're not going to look for it anymore?'

Sam stopped.

'You're putting me on the spot. I don't know. It's hard to prove anything with a negative.'

'By now it would have gone past the village and the school and through all this. Something should have happened,' said Maria.

'You should be pleased,' Anna chipped in. 'I know it nearly killed you but you won, there's no sign of it.'

At that moment a car passed them, turning from the road they were on into the bigger road that led to the car park. The car swung right without looking and a car coming the other way turned to avoid a collision and came straight at them. Brakes screeched and Sam grabbed both women and flung himself backwards into a narrow alleyway, dragging them with him. The car shuddered to a halt on the pavement where they had been standing. As Anna and Maria got to their feet Sam lay on his back not moving. Seconds later the drivers of the two cars came running up.

'Are you OK?' they both said at once.

Anna and Maria were still on their feet but Sam was flat out on the floor. He looked up at the two drivers. Both of them had blue eyes and all he could see in their faces was concern, no panic, no fear. He grinned and got to his feet.

'I'm fine,' he said. 'I'm enjoying a moment's rest.'

He dusted himself off, waited until the two cars had pulled away and turned to Maria.

'It has gone,' he said. 'I can feel it somehow, something in me has changed and do you know the best thing? When that car came at us, I didn't freeze.'

He leaned back against the wall and his face broke into a smile that seemed a mile wide.

'I didn't freeze.'

-- The End - -

QUESTIONS FOR BOOK GROUPS

It seems to be fashionable these days to have a section like this at the end of a book. I guess that one day there may even be standard or expected headings, but here are a few notes which have derived from conversations I have had with readers and some book groups.

Ley Lines

I have been somewhat cavalier in assigning properties to ley lines. The original work by Alfred Watkins simply suggested that they were ancient tracks and that the ancient peoples who used them marked them by utilising obvious landmarks in the landscape and adding standing stones, barrows and other man made artefacts, presumably to make it easier to follow the track. Watkins gave up calling them ley lines after a few years and referred to them as Old Straight Tracks.

Since Watkins's time, other writers have gone much further in giving the lines significance. Some believe they have energetic properties that can be identified by dowsing. Some have related them to astronomical observations which might have been used to predict the seasons or, of course, to navigate. Some theories appear even more outlandish and flying saucers, mythical aliens and other amazing or dark forces hover on the edge of the discussion.

It was not my intention to add more confusion to this area of debate but I have to say that after a few days reading material about ley lines on the Web I came to the conclusion that it was a game that anyone could play. The extent of the debate can be discovered through a small amount of research on the internet. I have not listed particular web sites for two reasons, both because such addresses often change and also because I do not want to appear to endorse any particular view of the existence or significance of ley lines.

Foot and Mouth disease

Most people will remember some of the awful scenes associated with getting the 2007 outbreak under control. I lived in rural Worcestershire at the time. We were not the worst affected county but for a number of weeks trucks carrying carcasses and others carrying fuel for pyres trundled past our house because we were on one of the routes from the motorway to a site where the remains of the slaughter were buried. That direct experience gave me a clear idea of the scale of the events and in addition I read a number of harrowing accounts on the Web. The enquiry after the event makes harrowing reading for many, especially those with links or interests in animals and the countryside. The story here is extracted, in what I hope is an anonymous way, from this body of evidence. It certainly appeared that in some cases inadequate manpower and lack of experience contributed to scenes that can only be described as horrific. I am not wishing to make any particular point that has not been made already, I was simply looking for a potentially plausible source for some kind of evil entity.

I hope that I have done justice to the memory of those events in creating a scary entity and giving it more power than mere memory.

Blue eyes

I refer to Professor Hans Eiberg from the Department of Cellular and Molecular Medicine at the University of Copenhagen. Simply putting Blue eyes + Hans Eiberg into Google brings up large numbers of references to his work. In *Aimless Fear* I simply add the suggestion that people with blue eyes have an additional talent that allows them to detect what is going on in ley lines.

I made that up. If I were to try to make the notion sound more believable I would say that ley lines and the belief in phenomena associated with them appear to be a mostly European idea and blue eyes are predominantly a European trait.

My apologies to anyone with blue eyes, or their friends. This is fiction. Do not worry about being overtaken by evil spirits, I made it up. I was simply looking for a device to make the thing only attack some people. If it affected everyone then it would be so much harder to collect evidence after each disaster. Events require witnesses, especially in novels. In this case the witnesses did not have blue eyes.

The characters

I have been remiss in many ways throughout the book in saying very little about what the characters look like, or for that matter in exploring their habits and foibles. I hope I have included or at least implied enough about each character that the reader can tell them apart. I have to admit that I simply find it more interesting to get on with the story so I only tend to include details that are likely to be germane to the plot.

A reader's group might like to discuss what they think the characters look like. Discussions could even be taken further by thinking about questions such as what sort of clothes do they wear, what do they have in their pockets, what music is on their iPod? These are the sorts of questions that writers are often asked to think about in creative writing classes when they develop characters. My apologies to anyone who runs such classes, I did think about it, I did make notes, I just didn't put them in the book.

Romance

Should there be some romance?

I hope that it is obvious that there is some affinity between Sam and Maria but I found it difficult to take this further because I could not believe that Sam would make an approach to a woman who had just lost her husband. He is not that kind of chap and of course he had the added issue of his freezing in crises, which inhibited him in any relationship that might be for the longer term. Sam was there, in what I hope was a tender moment when Maria identifies John's body at the morgue. He knows that she loved John and John's death is too recent.

One solution might have been to make the thing move more slowly, thus stretching the timeline and allowing long enough for some romance to evolve. I felt that would seem very artificial and would flatten the pace of the story and take away the urgency to solve the problem.

We are of course left with the question what happens next?

Some readers said that Maria should have been more upset. Let me assure everyone that she was dreadfully upset but she made sure that she didn't show it. There is a brief reference in Anna's chapter when she explains that she knows her mum is crying a lot. Those tears are shed in private. Maria is an experienced nursing sister and is modelled on a number of brilliant nurses and doctors that I worked with, all of who were very adept at keeping everything together when they were visible to patients, even when they were dreadfully upset or going through awful times in their own lives.

Jeopardy

Tradition has it, at least if you believe texts on creative writing, that the characters, especially the leading character must be in jeopardy. A common way in which this is achieved is through personal animosity between characters, with misunderstandings and sometimes downright malevolence getting in the way of the central problem being solved, or the MacGuffin being chased. For those who don't know what a MacGuffin is, I refer you to the internet; put MacGuffin (or McGuffin or maguffin) into your favourite search engine and you will be entertained. I find invented and unnecessary animosity tedious, so I sought to make all the jeopardy come from the nameless fear, which remains mysterious until the end. In particular I hoped to slightly surprise the reader by making the two 'fortune tellers' turn out, once their masks have slipped, to be rather sensible and agreeable people, who did not exploit Anna's vulnerability.

Does this work or would it have been a better story with more bad guys?

ABOUT THE AUTHOR

224

Professor Rod Griffiths CBE lives in Gloucestershire, UK and spends his time making up stories and trying to convince people that they might be true.

Some of the material in the book draws on his experience in medicine and public health, the rest is pure imagination.

www.ingramcontent.com/pod-product-compliance
Lightning Source LLC
Chambersburg PA
CBHW051500030726
47592CB00006B/2027

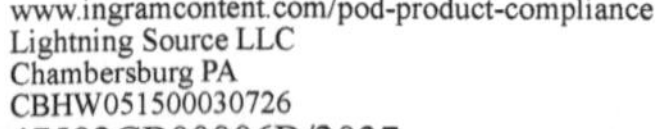